also by **ZACHARY LAZAR**

Evening's Empire

Sway

Aaron, Approximately

I PITY
THE POOR
IMMIGRANT

A NOVEL

ZACHARY LAZAR

Little, Brown and Company

NEW YORK   BOSTON   LONDON

Copyright © 2014 by Zachary Lazar

Little, Brown and Company
Hachette Book Group
237 Park Avenue, New York, NY 10017
littlebrown.com

First Edition: April 2014

Little, Brown and Company is a division of Hachette Book Group, Inc.
The Little, Brown name and logo are trademarks of Hachette Book Group, Inc.

Portions of this book appeared in *Bomb, The Southampton Review,* and *Fence.*

Photography credits: Benjamin Siegel, page 68; © Corbis; Meyer Lansky, page 68, © Hulton Archive/Getty. All other photographs are from the author's collection.

The publisher is not responsible for websites (or their content) that are not owned by the publisher.

The Hachette Speakers Bureau provides a wide range of authors for speaking events. To find out more, go to hachettespeakersbureau.com or call (866) 376-6591.

ISBN 978-0-316-25403-8
LCCN 2013954942

10 9 8 7 6 5 4 3 2 1

RRD-C

Printed in the United States of America

To Bill Clegg and Pat Strachan

I PITY
THE POOR
IMMIGRANT

"I'm not a kneeling Jew who comes to sing songs in your ears."

— **Meyer Lansky to
Senator Estes Kefauver, 1950**

1

Checking Out

NEW YORK, 2012

I remember taking my father to lunch at an Italian restaurant on 76th Street a few years ago, after my first book, a memoir of my brief marriage, had come out. It was October, and a waiter circulated among the tables with a plate of white truffles beneath a tiny bell jar so that when he lifted it you could take in the aroma before he shaved the truffles over small plates of risotto in black squid ink. Eighty dollars each, those small plates. I can recollect the pungent taste, the Sangiovese in our glasses. It was a daughter's gesture of affection or self-aggrandizement — these things were always murky between my father and me.

"You remember things," my father said. "I have the opposite problem. I live in the present too much."

It's been almost a year now since my father and I last saw each other. I should tell you that this is a recurring pattern in the story I'm about to tell — fathers and their children drifting apart, losing contact. Perhaps losing contact with my father was some unconscious fear or goal on my part when I flew to Israel for the first time in the spring of 2009 to investigate the murder of an Israeli writer named David Bellen. I went to cover Bellen's murder, but after my return I learned that the story led elsewhere. It led to a woman from my father's past named Gila Konig, who was born Tsilya Konig somewhere in Hungary, and who when I saw her briefly gave me her part of this story. Not that what she gave me was sufficient, only tantalizing. Gila Konig, like David Bellen, once lived in Tel Aviv. She is also now dead. My father isn't speaking to me anymore. These are some of the limitations of my sources for this new book.

Before his death, David Bellen said: "We don't choose our obsessions — our obsessions, invariably against our deepest wishes, choose us. Against our deepest wishes, we become suddenly, inexplicably, committed to a path we had avoided, a line of thought we'd had no interest in."

I once said in an interview: "What we need is a memoir without a self. A memoir about somebody other than 'me.' An understanding that the story of other people connected to 'me' might communicate more than the usual 'me,' might show the cultural context of 'me,' might even cast doubt on the viability of 'me.'"

I said this in the aftermath of a book scandal, another memoirist caught embellishing his or her "true story," telling lies. I'm quoting myself here with the same detachment with which I just quoted the writer David Bellen, who is one of the figures in what follows, this odd new "memoir" about people mainly other than "me." I don't know if any of this will make sense. What I mean is that the people in this story have become my story, or I have become their story. They are my proxies — I am imagining them as I imagine myself, both from a distance and from the inside. In writing this book, I have come to feel like a kind of immigrant in my own life, inhabiting a world of reflections and images of people I can't fully know, some of whom are dead, and I see now that my life has been shaped by this network, in ways I didn't always perceive.

A woman, Hannah Groff, goes on a journey. She's close to forty, divorced, without children, not unhappy but not what anyone would call "settled," a person in transit, on her way from New York to Tel Aviv to cover a murder. The journey starts with a crime and the crime ramifies, the woman finds she has dishonored people without quite intending to, including her father, who knew Gila Konig, who knew David Bellen, who wrote a book called *Kid Bethlehem* in which the biblical King David is presented in the guise of a twentieth-century gangster.

Gangsters are in this story too. They too are a part of who I've become.

Part One

Everywhere Present but Never Seen

2

Displaced Persons

TEL AVIV, 1972

Gila Konig looked at the photographs in the newspaper and
tried to connect them to the man she'd been secretly meeting this past year, but the pictures came from a different order of
reality. They were separate from what she knew about him — what
she thought she knew about him. His essential self was like his
body, which you could only take in one aspect at a time — the
belly, the slick gray hair, the small dark pupils of his eyes.

The photographs were in black and white — they were almost
kitsch, they were so old — and it required an effort of imagination to
see the violence in them as truly real. In one, a man was slumped
over on a floral print sofa in Beverly Hills. One of his eyes had been
shot out, his face a clown mask of gore. The blood blended with the
darkness of his necktie to cover half his chest in a dark stain. He had
been one of her lover's oldest and closest friends, Benjamin
Siegel — "Bugsy," the captions always called him. The nickname
served to cheapen his murder into something picaresque and quaint.

The next picture was also an antique — fifteen years ago, 1957. In

11

this one, there was little visible blood, just the body of a man flat on his back on a hairdresser's floor. His name was Albert Anastasia. He lay there in a near-cruciform position between two barber's chairs, his legs draped by a sheet and his head, shoulders, and arms by another sheet, or maybe they were towels. The only things exposed were an armpit, a chest covered in hair, a nipple, an outstretched hand.

The photos and the words were sensational — that is, they managed to paradoxically both magnify and diminish their subjects. The Meyer she knew was calm, not friendly, fastidiously clean, strategic. There was a reason, she thought, that his body had never turned up in a tabloid newspaper photograph.

On the ride into Tel Aviv, he noticed that the sidewalks were full of people looking up at the sky. His driver came off Kings of Israel Square — the city hall like an assemblage of cheap building blocks, pigeons in the big asphalt emptiness — and suddenly everything was cast in shadow. Outside the cafés, waiters stood at the edges of mostly empty tables, arms crossed over their pressed shirts. Right on Frishman, past Dizengoff, Ben Yehuda — juice stands, falafel, laundromats — then farther toward the beach, where the concierges had come out of the hotels, peering and twisting, finding it. Crowds of people silently looking up at the sky, not looking at the car, not looking at him. They turned to each other over their shoulders, then went back to watching what was above, then slowly resumed their courses, heads still raised. There was no way to see from the car what they were looking at.

"What's happening?" Lansky finally asked the driver.

"I don't know," the driver said. "There must be an eclipse. Something like that."

He spoke fluent English, though with an Israeli accent that at times sounded oddly German.

"I read the paper this morning," Lansky said. "There was nothing about an eclipse."

"Clouds maybe."

"Maybe a patch of clouds. Not an eclipse."

A crowd of men in suits stood outside the lobby doors, the driveway two lanes thick with black cars. Everyone kept looking at the sky. Lansky waited in the backseat while the driver went in to clear his way. He saw his bag sitting in the sun on the bellman's cart. The driver returned and he got out of the car, and he and the driver walked past the doorman into the brown lobby. The driver nodded as Lansky got into the elevator by himself and the doors closed.

Gila was sitting in a chair, smoking, still in her uniform, slumped like a child in the beige blouse and black skirt, black nylons. Instead of looking at him, she closed her eyes and exhaled.

"Yosha took my shift," she said. "I need the money, but it's okay. What is bad is the way she makes me grovel for it. She knows I'm coming up here, so she makes me grovel."

He looked over at the bar, the ice bucket, the tongs. "You shouldn't be begging around like that. You shouldn't be working here at all."

"I should be in Ramat Gan, shopping for a new Mercedes. Is that what your wife drives?"

He nodded absently or dismissively and walked toward the window. Beneath them was the Mediterranean, Hayarkon Promenade, the beach with its spatter of orange umbrellas, green umbrellas, swimmers standing in the shallows. Everything was ordinary — the sun had come back out. He went to the bar and made them both a drink.

"I drove into town and all the sudden it was very cloudy," he said. "Like an eclipse, that was how cloudy it was. Everyone looking up. The whole way down here, I'm worrying how I would get in the hotel without everyone seeing, all the cameras lately, but everyone was just watching the sky. There weren't any cameras anyway. It was just luck — the clouds, no cameras. My whole life I said that people who believed in luck, they lose, period. Fate, luck, whatever. I guess you can't really get away from it."

She was taking off her shoes. He watched, sipping his drink. She knew he was watching. She looked up at him, bent forward, her hair falling in her eyes.

"Where will you go if they make you leave?" she said.

"What makes you think I'll have to leave?"

"Fate, luck. Those are dangerous words. Maybe you should go back to Poland, that would give them a surprise."

"You should watch your mouth."

"Watch my mouth."

"Whatever comes into your head, you just say it. Maybe that's why you're still serving cocktails at a hotel."

His luggage arrived, five identical changes of clothes. He was tipping the bellman when she put on the bracelet he'd brought her. She looked at it in the mirror, a line bracelet of white gold and small diamonds. Her drink sat untouched on the nightstand. He watched her look at the bracelet and he knew she was already thinking about where to sell it.

Tel Aviv — the sun reflected by water, the coolness between you and it when you looked out the window. The run-down buildings, concrete and stripped paint, the fish lunch in Jaffa, crumbling by the sea.

She had grown up partly in Foehrenwald, a DP camp not far from Munich. Before that, ten months in Bergen-Belsen. When she and her mother came to Israel, her mother changed her name from Tsilya to Gila. It meant "happiness." He looked at the flatness of her stomach, her breasts, the faint shadows along her rib cage. Sometimes it was beyond him, an effort of patience, but now he relaxed, slow, cognizant, closing his eyes. The sound of her name and the sight of her body as he let his eyes come open again.

───────

Gangster, racketeer, mobster — she could not get the words to adhere to the physical person. Not that she disbelieved the stories, but the stories' language glared, whereas the truth of him resided in understatement. The gray trousers and the pressed shirt, white linen or pale blue linen. The leather shoes and the blue blazer and the *Herald Tribune*. Everything important was invisible, maybe glimpsed for just an instant when he turned to her in a certain way and his eyes accused her of looking too closely.

Albert Anastasia had been shot ten times, one of the shots blowing open his skull. Ben "Bugsy" Siegel sprawled in death as if napping on the sofa, his jacket lapel turned up toward his neck, as if he had sought warmth against the onslaught, blood gushing from his eye. Both of them killers before being killed. Both of them Meyer's partners or vassals or something. She wondered how much of a killer you had to be for others to do your killing for you, to be that separate from the particulars, if that was the truth about him.

A proliferation of rumors, he would say, rumors and lies. He had come to Israel seeking a reprieve from all that — the FBI tail, the false indictments, the subpoenas, the attorney's fees. In a life-time of scrutiny, he had never been convicted of a serious crime. That was why he had come here, because they were supposed to accept even someone like him. As a Jew, even he had the right of return, the birthright of Israeli citizenship.

They drove the hour from Tel Aviv barely talking, the journalist watching the road, sleeves rolled back on his tanned arms. His name was Uri Dan; he was a military correspondent, a sympathetic ear, according to Lansky's lawyer, Yoram Alroy. Dan had long black hair, a Swiss watch, a chalk-striped shirt half unbuttoned in the heat. An ability to tolerate silence, the first sign of poise.

They parked near the InterContinental Hotel amid the tour buses and stood for a few minutes by the rail with the crowd. Below them, the Mount of Olives was a huge lunar space of white stone, white sand, dark gray cedar trees, the cemetery descending like a dusty quarry cut in steps. The old graves looked like part of the hill-side, eternal, sloping down in endless terraces toward the Valley of Jehoshaphat, where the dead would rise. Above it glowed the Old City of Jerusalem — the gold Dome of the Rock, the crenellated wall, the remnants of David's ancient kingdom, covered over now by the Arab district of Silwan, run-down, cubist, hung with laundry.

Dan squinted down at the cemetery. "It's unfortunate, the neglect," he said, raising a flat hand at the panorama. "There's never enough money to restore it, and once you restore some of it, the boys come down from East Jerusalem and smash it to bits again."

"Arabs," Lansky said.

"Yes, of course, Arabs."

A photographer said hello in English and took their photograph.

"You don't mind?" Dan said, turning his head.

Lansky bowed and lit a cigarette. He shook out the lit match, then slid the book back inside the lower pocket of his blazer, pushing it down behind the flap with two fingers. "I'm not crazy about it," he said. "I'm not really crazy about any of this."

He had explained himself to Dan back in Tel Aviv, how he hoped Dan might write a more balanced account of who he was and why he was here, something to counter the tabloids. His grandparents were buried in Jerusalem — when life had become impossible in Grodno, his grandparents had come here to Jerusalem, while he and his family had gone to New York. He had not been able to find their graves before. Maybe Dan could help him — maybe that was a way they could begin the conversation.

They started down the steep hill, the scenery blinding. They passed the Church of the Ascension, Christian tour groups in the Garden of Gethsemane. The olive trees with their scarred trunks looked like enormous hunks of driftwood. *Benjamin Suchowljansky, plot 15, column B, grave 80.* His grandfather Benjamin, whom he had last seen sixty years ago, when the languages he spoke were Polish and Yiddish and he was nine years old.

Dogs wandered among the rocks, the broken gates, the weeds. A decrepit rabbi had led them to the grave, where he bent down and cleaned the dirty inscription with his coat sleeve. Lansky pushed his sunglasses back over his head and wiped his eyes. He looked out across the valley without seeing anything but the brightness. He saw his grandfather in a full-length coat, beard, fur-trimmed hat. The dim shul with its broken Torah scrolls decaying on the shelves. The smell of the spice box, the moldy smell of men among books, the *yahrtzeit* candle in its glass. In Tel Aviv, you never thought about these things, you lived in 1972. He saw himself at twelve, smashing a plate in someone's face — whores on Madison Street, *shtarkes* and pimps. New York faces crammed beneath the awnings, wagons and pushcarts and rain.

He took his sunglasses all the way off and held them folded in his hand. He closed his eyes and said the prayer for the dead, remembering the foreign words from three or four lifetimes ago.

"Before we left Poland, there was a big argument," he said to no one in particular. "I was nine years old, so I remember. My grandfather wanted to be buried here in Israel — he was already an old man. My father wanted all of us to go to America. He thought there would be opportunity there — the old story. Opportunity. In Grodno, one day the rabbi came across a dead girl in the woods, a Polish girl, she'd been raped and killed. So the rabbi ran back for help and they said it must have been him who killed her. He wanted her blood for the Passover — that's what they said. They cut him up into pieces while he was still alive. They took the four pieces of his body and they nailed them to the city walls of Grodno. It was a brave thing just to take them down and give him a proper burial. We left in 1911, and my parents and my brother and I went to New York and my grandparents came here. My grandfather wanted to die here, just like I want to die here. Die here as a Jew."

He gave the rabbi some money and asked him to look after the graves, then they walked back up the hill. It was hot and he took off his jacket. Poland, New York — the places of his life had begun to lose their meaning. Their meaning was subsumed by this landscape, religious and shaming. The light was honey colored and the dirt and the trees looked the same way they had looked five thousand years ago. Uri Dan walked through it all like an insouciant guide, watching his feet on the rocks, a native-born Israeli, a sabra, not just a Jew.

If only he had come here in 1911, instead of going to New York. The barked orders as they boarded the *Kursk*, the ignorant silence, food sloshing by in wooden buckets. Seasick, he would walk the decks and look at the people sitting there like pack animals in their blankets and rags.

They drove through the Lions' Gate and walked across the Muslim Quarter to the Western Wall. Paper yarmulkes lay in piles on the card tables. Tufts of weeds grew out of the stones in extravagant bushes. He stood in front of the wall with his sunglasses in his shirt pocket, pressing the bridge of his nose, eyes closed. Beside him a boy in a white shawl bowed in rhythm, a prayer book in his hands. Lansky touched his forehead to the stone. You couldn't take it all in, what it cost in blood.

United States District Court

FOR THE

Southern District of Florida

United States of America

V.

MEYER LANSKY

To The United States Marshal or any other authorized agent or officer

You are hereby commanded to arrest MEYER LANSKY and bring him forthwith before the United States District Court for the Southern District of Florida in the city of Miami to answer to an Indictment charging him with

Criminal Contempt, in that he refused to appear before the United States Grand Jury in the Southern District of Florida on March 10 and 11, 1971, pursuant to lawful subpoena and court order in violation of Title 18, U.S.C. Section 401

Dated at Miami, Florida
on March 24th 1971
Bail fixed at $200,000 SURETY

When he hadn't returned, they'd revoked his U.S. passport. Extradite him, was the Department of Justice's message to Israel. LANSKY, ACCORDING TO DE CARLO, HAS A "PIECE" OF VIRTUALLY EVERY CASINO IN LAS VEGAS DUE TO HIS EARLY ENTRY AS THE "PROTECTION" FOR JEWISH ELEMENT WHO ORGANIZED GAMBLING ELEMENT THERE. HE LISTED FLAMINGO, DESERT INN, STARDUST, SANDS, AND FREMONT AS HOTELS IN WHICH LANSKY HAS INTEREST. The Department of Justice had so much intelligence on him that they no longer knew what was fact and what was myth. Of course it was in his nature that they would never know.

Later, Uri Dan would write that even before he met Lansky he was opposed to those Israeli authorities who wanted to send him back to the U.S. He would write, "On principle I defended his right as a Jew to come and live in the land of his ancestors." He would go further: "Israelis had been molded by blood, violence, and a struggle for survival and power in the sands of the Middle East." Lansky had used his connections to help arm the Haganah during Israel's fight for independence. He and his men had broken up Nazi rallies in Yorkville in the 1930s. "He fascinated me," Dan wrote. "Meyer Lansky has that type of personality."

The allure of power, the allure even of its excesses. Of course it is the excesses that account for the allure. Some negative force everywhere present but never seen. The black-and-white photographs of murdered gangsters. Meyer Lansky walking his shih tzu near the beach on Tel Aviv's Hayarkon Promenade.

———————

He uncapped the Pernod, listening to Gila translate the article from the Hebrew. It was the usual life summary. He tried to listen, displeased even by the facts once they'd been presented in the funhouse mirror of someone else's language. No serious criminal convictions — was it because he was innocent, or because of his shrewd invisibility? He had spent the last forty years not commenting on these things. He looked Gila in the eye when she got to the murders of Ben Siegel and Albert Anastasia. He sipped his drink and waited for her to start reading again and then he turned away and listened, staring at the wall.

"I liked Dan all right," he finally said. "The more I talked to him, the more I did. Very smart. Very close with Ariel Sharon. He's covered Sharon for fifteen years."

"Sabras," she said. Her voice was distant, somewhere between a hiss and a sigh. "Big balls like an ox, at least that's what they think. They spit on people like me. Refugees."

She was still contemplating the story. It had become more interesting than he was. He stood by the window and looked out at the beach, crowded even at sunset. The coolness of the Pernod on his tongue, the herbal sweetness. He fished for his cigarettes in the pocket of his robe.

"I guess they taught you pretty good English at that DP camp," he said.

"English. Dressmaking. Lots of things."

"A real finishing school. Dressmaking."

"We made dresses and the boys made watches. Useful Jews. We loved the Americans, they were very patient with us. Then we come here and there's no work, nothing to eat. Lentils, a few cucumbers."

He exhaled the cigarette and started coughing. Gila folded up the newspaper and laid it on the bed.

"I couldn't save my friend Ben Siegel," he said, still facing the window. "He had that kind of temperament — he liked a fight. He thought he could cheat people, even the goddamn Italians, and they would back down. I never backed down, but I always used my head. It's easy to blow yourself up. It happened to Ben, it happened to a lot of people I worked with in those days. The wheel turned, they lost. Not that they were animals, but they were characters, personalities. I used to take a lot of crap for being quiet. I was quiet. I wasn't any better than they were, but I was quiet."

He looked at the newspaper on the bed. In English, the title was *Meyer Lansky Breaks His Silence*. Some kind of raffish joke, a stereotype from an old movie. FLAMINGO, DESERT INN, STARDUST, SANDS, AND FREMONT. Useful Jews. Everything secret, everything always at risk. Now Ben was long dead, he himself was sixty-nine. If they made him leave, he didn't know where he'd go.

———

He walked with his two lawyers through the crowd past the concrete planters full of weeds. The Palace of Justice was in a shabby part of modern Jerusalem near some defunct railroad tracks, the sidewalks hemmed in by dented chain-link fence. Amid the fans and the dark wooden beams, he tried to follow the rhetoric. His Israeli lawyer, Alroy, made an argument in Hebrew, then the State of Israel's lawyer, Gavriel Bach, made a counterargument in Hebrew. For once, he was not asked to speak. He sat beside his American lawyer, Rosen, and the two of them read along as an interpreter translated on a yellow pad with a ballpoint pen. The five supreme court justices listened to the contradictions. He was the head of the Mafia and had a fortune of three hundred million dollars. He was a retired hotel operator and had practically no money at all. It was theater — the robed judges, the lawyers rising and sitting back down. If he was the kind of outlaw they alleged he was, then the only legitimate response would be silence. Either he was guilty of everything and it couldn't be proved, or he was guilty of nothing and it couldn't be proved.

The State of Israel in its twenty-four years had taken in hundreds of thousands of Jewish victims in the service of ending forever the saga of Jewish victimhood. He had ended his own victimhood a long time ago, before Israel existed. There were Israelis, many of whom had fought in wars, who believed that the end justified the means. There were others, many of whom had fought in wars, who believed otherwise.

He had attracted a large following now. The cameras would be there waiting for the next recess, Lansky out smoking in the courtyard with its scraggly palm trees, surrounded by young men who had come to see him. He would sit on a bench or on the steps and look at the restaurant sign across the street with its two red Coca-Cola logos, and he could have been in Miami facing trial there.

Mr. Lansky, what is the Jewish Mafia?

Mr. Lansky, have you ever committed a violent crime?

Mr. Lansky, are you a religious Jew?

Mr. Lansky, who killed Bugsy Siegel?

He didn't answer — sometimes he made a joke. After five days, the hearings were over. Fate, luck, whatever. Whatever happened was out of his hands.

―――――

Gila wondered sometimes if she wanted him to be worse than he was. As if to be worse was also to be stronger, and somehow by association for her to be stronger.

She had brought her sketches to show a man named Gelb — he mostly did swimwear — and he muttered about which factories could make the stitch, private labels, things she already knew, industry talk. He had some acquaintance on Seventh Avenue who did knockoffs of big couture lines, maybe he could put her in touch. The offer was not so much mechanical as scornful. Swimwear, when she designed women's clothes. Seventh Avenue, when she was in Tel Aviv.

Her mother napped in the reclining chair, hands like wax, her head covered by a bright orange scarf like some Orthodox housewife. If you had the choice between illness and death, you chose illness. Radiation and chemo, hope and despair. Her mother was younger than Meyer.

She watched him on TV. He looked terrible, weak, except for his eyes, standing in a slouch outside the Palace of Justice, cigarette in hand. Just from looking at him you could tell he had lost the case — he would have to leave Israel now. When he spoke, he reminded people that only a week ago, in Munich, terrorists had kidnapped and murdered eleven athletes from Israel's Olympic team. He spoke of it in a strangely poetic way. *Young branches cut down,* were the words he chose. Young branches: by comparison his loss meant very little. He was an old man with a weak chin and a sunken mouth. She tried to see him that way.

He stared at the Old City of Jerusalem from a window of the King David Hotel. It would be a maze of narrow alleys this late at night — Armenian restaurants, souks, cracked buildings where everyone lived in a different century. From his room he could see the crenellated wall lit up like a theme park, the Tower of David with its parapets and flag. Egypt would come from the west, Syria from the north — everyone knew it was just a matter of time. You waited for the city to explode, but it didn't. It glowed like something in a nightmare.

They ate in a café up the beach from the Dan Hotel, rows of tables and wicker chairs, oil lamps in glass boxes. Hummus, olives, tabouleh, labneh, baba ghanoush. The moon shone on the water. It was still a shock to have people's eyes on her when she was with him. She tilted her head back to sip the cold beer from the large glass. He was watching her eat, sitting back a little from the table, smoking.

"I remember when you first came into the lobby," she said. "People talked about you already. Who is he, he's someone famous. You would just sit by yourself, drinking coffee, very quiet. Very calm."

"No one special."

"Like you owned the world."

He bowed his head, turning the cigarette slowly in his fingers. "We could go to Caesarea for a couple days. Or maybe just stay here, relax."

"I like Caesarea."

She smiled down at her food, but the quiet way she said it was a way of saying no. They never spoke about her mother or her illness. She wondered how he was able to come and go so easily when he lived with his wife.

The room was blue in the dark and he lay on his back with his fists against his temples, waiting for it to pass. There were times when he couldn't do much of anything and it made him pound the bed in anger and shame. It was their last time together. He let his hand rest on her thigh and she held it there.

"I'm going to make a Pernod," she said. "Would you like one too?"

"Yes, fine."

"Just one ice cube to make it turn milky."

They sipped their drinks and didn't speak. Afterward, he lay with his head on her bare stomach. He was clean and he smelled like cologne, and he moved himself up and they stayed that way for a long time. She had to concentrate — he was concentrating too — they went slowly. His body was not unpleasant. It was a yearning body, and she held him closely in her arms.

They slept late the next morning and then they said goodbye.

———

She was a cocktail waitress. Businessmen, scotch and gin, some stale pastries in a glass case, no music in the background. One night, after Meyer had left Israel, the journalist Uri Dan came in with a group from the embassies, and he half stood and pointed at each of them with his cigarette, relaying their orders, not seeing her. Of course, he could not have known who she was. Of course, she was nobody. She bent at the knees, serving, back straight, focused on the glasses, the table. The inventedness of Israel as a country seemed completely transparent at such moments, everything too new to be convincing, but she realized that this was a refugee's thinking. The real problem was that she had never gotten used to the newness, had never taken her position in the country seriously enough.

She was smoking at the bar in her uniform one day when Meyer's driver walked into the lobby in his jeans and sunglasses. He had come to check on her and also to give her something — he would explain it to her in the car if she had a few minutes to go for a drive. She remembered him, they had met a few times before.

They left the hotel driveway and started up Frishman Street, past Ben Yehuda, Dizengoff, the sudden open space of Kings of Israel Square — pigeons and litter, discount stores fronted by cafés with white tables. They kept east until it got quieter, a neighborhood of modern apartment buildings, flowering trees, benches in the shade. The lantana grew in hedges, its pink and orange petals dusting the sidewalks like scraps of bright plastic.

"This is where he lived," the driver said. "Here and in Ramat Gan. He lived in a lot of places."

She stared at his turned face.

"He said the rent would be taken care of. I told him I would take you here and give you the keys. You can do whatever you want after that."

She sat there looking at it through the window, the narrow walkway up to the glass door beside the post boxes. It was a gray building like a thousand others in Tel Aviv, built on concrete stilts so cars could be parked beneath it. Inside, there was a tiny elevator with a brass gate that you had to pull back by hand before the door would close. There was barely enough room for the two of them. On the third floor, they exited into a dim hallway with a linoleum floor, mezuzahs on the identical doorframes, a smell of cabbage. It was smaller than her own hallway. It looked like a place to die.

Another war broke out — on Yom Kippur, Egypt and Syria attacked from the west and the north, in Sinai and the Golan Heights. It meant long weeks of sitting in the TV light, warming soup or just tea, bathing her mother, skeletal and bruised. The city would disappear, the country would disappear, bodies amid the shredded cars and buildings. She wanted to leave, to move to New York, but her mother kept living and so for a long time she forgot about her ambitions and her plans.

The war ended. She read that in Miami, Meyer had been acquitted of all charges: contempt, conspiracy, tax evasion. She felt certain now that it was not because he was innocent but because his life had been lived so invisibly. No one knew who he was, neither had she. Every once in a while she went back to the apartment to see that it was still there, still waiting for her. Three empty rooms with marks on the bare white walls from where the furniture had stood, where the pictures had hung. Broken slats in the closet door. The water in the kitchen sink would sputter out brown until it ran clear. Such a strange, unwanted gift, as if he were finally telling her something crucial. *The future will not be much different from now. Tsilya. Gila. Look at the odds.*

3

Only Connect

NEW YORK, 2012

A memoir without a self. A memoir about someone other than "me." An understanding that the story of other people connected to "me" might communicate more than the usual "me," might show the cultural context of "me," might even cast doubt on the viability of "me."

I remember being in Florida to cover a murder case you may have heard about because it involves the infamous lobbyist Jack Abramoff. The case had been tied up in court since 2005. When it went to trial, Abramoff was not expected to appear, though he had of course been convicted of other crimes for which he'd served forty-three months in federal prison. He'd appeared at his previous trial in a dark trench coat and fedora, like a gangster from decades ago. In news stories, he was sometimes likened to Meyer Lansky.

When Gila first told me her story in the spring of 2010, I knew almost nothing about Meyer Lansky and wasn't very interested in him or in the lore surrounding him. It was the women in his life, starting with Gila, that made me interested.

From the *New York Times*, June of 1995:

> Hannah M. Groff, daughter of Lawrence H. Groff, of New York, NY, is to be married today to John V. Haynes, the son of Dr. and Mrs. Donald Haynes, of East Hampton, NY. The civil ceremony will take place at the Hayneses' home in East Hampton with a reception to follow.
>
> Ms. Groff, 25, is a recent graduate of the journalism school at Columbia University. Mr. Haynes, 28, is a litigation associate at Byrons and Company, a New York law firm.

I remember when I was young, hearing a song called "The Adultress," about a woman, like Gila, who loses herself in secrets. The singer, Chrissie Hynde, seemed like the kind of woman I might be someday, the kind of woman I thought I wanted to be someday — the song seemed autobiographical. Later, when I became something like that kind of woman, I had long since forgotten the model for the role I was playing, though by then it might have occurred to me that the song was less a boast than an indictment. The song had come out the year I first met Gila, 1981, though I didn't hear it until much later. I had mostly forgotten Gila by then. I had forgotten how much she'd meant to me when I was young, though some shadow of her must have always been there.

Nathanael West writes: *It is hard to laugh at the need for beauty and romance, no matter how tasteless, even horrible, the results of that need are. But it is easy to sigh.*

Frankie Lymon asks, *Why do fools fall in love?*

home n. *a place of residence or refuge, as in the Promised Land, Tomorrowland, Never Never Land.*

I'll tell you one more story about the women in Meyer Lansky's life before I tell you about myself. One more story about a woman who loses herself in secrets.

4

Immigrants, Part 1

New York, 1928–29

I

She touched up her lipstick in the powder room mirror, a girl who'd sewn her own dress from a Butterick pattern, a blue shift she wore with a brooch of fake pearls — Anne Citron, formerly Anna — the name change a hopeful step away from the past, a step toward here, the Park Central Hotel. The beige light settled behind her on a grouping of cane chairs on a pale carpet. Her face in the mirror seemed too long, the curves Semitic. The longer she stood taking in the room's stillness, the more haughty and derisive it became.

She left the nickel Meyer had given her in the attendant's basket and went back into the dining room. At her place on the table was a small velvet box. The whole night so far had felt illicit — American, unfamiliar, not Jewish. Now he was giving her a ring, as in the movies.

She looked at him and his eyes changed and she looked back

down, trying to smile, imagining the way it ought to appear. He prodded her to open the box. She didn't know whether to sit or keep standing, so she sat clumsily back in the chair. The ring's small size surprised her — the smallness made it less dreamlike. It was a round crystal set in what she imagined at first was silver. Only gradually did she understand that it wasn't silver and it wasn't a crystal.

He looked at her with his mouth parted, eyes mistrusting. She was worried now in a way that was almost superstitious.

"Is it paste or is it real?" she asked.

"That's a diamond."

"Meyer."

"That's a real diamond."

There was something flummoxed about how he adjusted himself in his chair. "I shouldn't have surprised you like that."

He had reached across the table and taken back the box. He snapped it closed with a quiet movement of his index finger, then secreted it away in the lower pocket of his jacket.

"Does it mean what I think it means?" she asked.

"That's a real diamond. You think about it for a couple days, then you tell me what you think it means."

On the table between them were stemmed glasses, white dishes, silverware arrayed on the white cloth — whiteness and high spaces full of air. He wished she would sit up straighter, not be so dour and scared. The waiter brought over two cut-glass dishes filled with diced melon and pineapple — fruit cocktails, they were called. It was Prohibition, so there was no wine.

"I heard you drove all the way to Florida," she said later in the backseat of the dark car. They were in a garage on Cannon Street that he and Ben Siegel owned, among a fleet of other cars that he and Ben owned.

"I never drove to Florida," he said.

"Were there storks there?"

"Who told you that?"

"Not storks, pelicans. Flamingos."

"I never drove to Florida. I never drove anywhere near that far."

He felt the neckline of her dress against his wrists, her face in his hands, the length and fineness of her hair. She was warm on top of the opened coat. He had worried at first that it would be strange that she was taller than he was, but instead there was a sense of abundance. He kissed her and moved his hands toward her breasts and she pushed them away, over and over, as slow and repetitive as the waves on a lake.

The crowd filed out and they stayed seated, the soft light on the theater's Moorish columns, her hand on his coat sleeve. The movie's spell was tenuous and she knew it, and she wanted it to last longer. It had been a college movie: an America of football, a dog rolling on the grass, a blond boy with a row of white teeth scoring the winning touchdown, his cheering friends in V-neck sweaters and ties. The lightest froth, so silly and glowing that the actors spoofed themselves, opening their eyes a little too wide at the camera, screwing up their smiles with a devious slant, but she could see by looking at Meyer in the dark that he didn't scoff, that he'd been infected by it. Donald Keith, aroused by girls but unable to articulate anything; Clara Bow, "The Hot Potato," a wild girl with a dark bob and teasing eyes. You watched the callow boy grow into his infatuation and the girl echo each of his changes

with her own. *If there's a moon tonight, do you want to take a walk?*
Moonlight indicated by a blue filter, daylight in sepia. The lovers
went to a speakeasy with checkered tablecloths, the hall jammed
to the rafters with dancing couples, a funny old black woman flip-
ping pancakes on a griddle, stealing a bottle of gin when the cops
raided. A college movie — "Prescott College." The sadness of
graduation. How Donald Keith had changed so much in his four
undergraduate years, from an awkward boy to a hale, confident
man. He slapped down some cad who tried to kiss Clara Bow
against her wishes, and in this way, as well as in his awkwardness,
Donald Keith was like Meyer.

They sat at joined tables — the Lanskys and her family, the Cit-
rons — her brother Jules in a silk tie and beige suit, across from
him Meyer's mother staring absently through thick lenses. Waiters
in vests brought blintzes, sour cream, whitefish, borscht. She
watched the plates go by without appetite. She knew so many
things now. How the garage on Cannon Street was more than just
a garage. How Meyer and Ben owned property like it all over the
city and in New Jersey and Philadelphia. How they imported
whiskey from Scotland on ships they chartered themselves and
then distributed it across the United States to wealthy businessmen, even politicians. Her friend Esta, Ben's girl, had told her
this. Esta, the brassy one, her lips clenched in the moment before
she burst forth with the secrets, what Ben had told her after their
date at the French Bakers or Manny Wolf's restaurant, the movie,
or the pleasure drive in the Gardner coupe or the Dodge Brothers
sedan.

    She watched her father frown his way through two plates of
food, a squat man in a scuffed hat. Meyer bowed his head and

didn't speak, the lunch a duty to be gotten through. When it was over, he reached into his pants pocket and discreetly gave one of the waiters money without asking for a bill, placing his hand on the man's shoulder as he bent down. Everyone saw, had been waiting for it. Her father endured the moment with a scheming stare at the dish of cream that still remained on the table. She had never imagined her father capable of jealousy. As they were getting up to go, he took Meyer aside and they talked in the tiny space between the table and the bathroom, Meyer's topcoat draped over his arm, a young man with money, an old man giving him trite advice.

"He asked if I wanted a job," Meyer told her afterward. "Out in Hoboken at the store. I said of course, sure, I'd be honored."

She turned, holding him in her squint. They were parked outside the tenements they'd both grown up in, bedding slung from the fire escapes. A thick crowd parted passively around the car with their bundles and sacks, none of them looking in the windows, Anne in her old Butterick dress, Meyer in his coat and hat and gloves.

"I'll help him with the accounting, the books. A couple days a week. He's your father."

She looked down at the ring on her finger. For a startled moment she'd pictured Meyer standing at the counter in an apron. Already she'd begun to imagine an apartment far uptown with high windows, carpets, chandeliers. Not just to imagine it but to think of it as rightfully hers.

Buds on the trees as they crossed the Hudson and followed the highway north into Westchester, Rockland, Orange. The cliffs sheared down to the river, the great pale trees growing in the ledges of the rock. She had never seen so much space, so much light. They drove all the way to the Canadian border, through a wilderness without buildings. America — a honeymoon. A girl from a tenement with a damp latrine in the hall, a common sink, floorboards shiny with kitchen scraps and muck.

II

A fifth of Dewar's, bought for two dollars, sold for more than thirty — a fifteen hundred percent profit when just the year before the Dewar's had been legal. A fifteen hundred percent profit on something more and more people openly wanted, and you were eighteen and you had left school to work in a tool-and-die shop for ten cents an hour, fifty-two hours a week. Three thousand speakeasies in New York City alone. In Grodno, his mother had taken music lessons. They had lived in a stone house in the center of town. Bright lights in the machine shop, the thud of the punches, men in coveralls at the lathes.

III

He stood and took the call in the suite's bedroom, pressing his free ear shut with two fingers, looking at the dark blue of the windows on the south side of Central Park. He made a visor of his hand against the glass and saw the damp streets in the lamplight. It was Anne again, saying she thought the baby was coming.

"It's very early," he said. "It's three months early."

"You don't understand. It's coming now."

"You're not bleeding, are you?"

"Meyer."

He lit a cigarette and scanned the nightstand for the ashtray. He told her he'd be home in a few minutes, then he hung up. In the next room, they were all seated among the furniture, the pale linen wallpaper, the silver service trays on the sideboard and the low table. He looked past the men in their hats to the front hallway with its chandelier and vases, like the foyer of a town house.

"You look pale," his friend Charlie Luciano said. His white shirt was ample, brilliantly clean, and with the sleeves rolled up and the collar open without a tie it implied an abundance of other shirts just like it or even finer.

"She's having a rough time," Meyer said.

"What other kind of time is there?"

They went back into the bedroom to speak in private. They spoke almost entirely in numbers, the floor lamp in the corner casting its stale halo of light over the wing chair.

"Not much discussion in the other room," Charlie said. "Even if they're talking out there now, they're not really thinking about anything but that closed door, us on the other side of it."

"I'm not worried about them," Meyer said.

"They're making money."

"Even Anastasia. Genovese."

"They've got their qualities. It's just that they're not good ones."

They were all Italians in the other room. Unlike Charlie, most of them never denied how much they liked the taste in their mouths of the word "kike."

She was standing in her nightgown at the stove. He watched from the doorway in his hat and coat, having called out her name and received no answer. A bare bulb hung from a coil in the ceiling and shone down on her back, her feet swelling over the edges of her slippers.

She shivered and convulsed against his chest, his hands on her shoulders. Holding her now was unsexual, confusing, hopeless. The milk on the stove was starting to boil. He didn't know how to get through to the moment when he could let her go and shut off the flame. Instead, she turned away from him and threw the pot across the kitchen at the wall.

She'd thought the baby had died that August, ten weeks in. Her breasts weren't tender anymore, she wasn't queasy — in the bedroom she'd looked at her bare stomach and started weeping, afraid at first to even touch it. She'd called him home and he'd taken her to the doctor and the doctor said it was common, everything was fine, but then the worrying began. In the humid August days, she would lie in bed with a damp cloth on her face and a fan set on a chair, falling in and out of sleep, the plate of toast on the sheets beside her, the fan watching like a metal eye. The nausea returned. He didn't know what to do for her. She would sit on the edge of the bed as if she was trying to imagine standing up.

A small temporary place in Brooklyn. He was superstitious in this way — you couldn't set up a baby's room until it was born and safe and you knew it would be all right. He went even further. Until the baby was born, they would live in a two-room apartment in Brooklyn with plaid chairs and a broken radio and someone else's books on the shelves.

He'd fallen asleep in the sitting room and so he was still dressed when the door buzzer went off around 3:00 a.m. He met Ben Siegel in the stairway and Ben looked up, his tie pulled to one side between the lapels of his double-breasted suit. A thin blond beard showed in blotches at his sideburns and cheeks, almost an adolescent's beard.

"They didn't call you?" he said.

"No."

"They said they called. I said if they called, why didn't they talk to you?"

Meyer shook his head and indicated that they should go back downstairs to the foyer to talk. When Ben got too loud, Meyer nudged him toward the door and they went out on the stoop in the cold air. Nothing about what he said sounded true — as he told the story even Ben began to realize this. Charlie Luciano had disappeared. Someone should have called Meyer hours ago but they hadn't called him. Vito Genovese should have called.

They went into the apartment so he could get his things. Anne was stooped forward in the kitchen with her crossed arms at her breasts, still hardly awake, tangled hair rising above her head. The spattered milk had almost dried on the wall. He looked at her and walked into the sitting room. The lamp with its tasseled shade cast a pale glow on the curtains, the plaid chairs, the *Daily Mirror* stacked on the floor. He put his tie back on and smoothed his hair with his hands, then he took the homburg off its block and put it on. He was working the combination of the safe when he turned to find her in the archway. She was staring at him, only faintly confused now. Ben came up behind her.

"Never leave an Irishman in charge," he said. "This Scanlon goes out for a pleasure drive, two o'clock a.m., the *shvantz* forgets the keys to the garage."

She pushed him away, turning to Meyer. "What's going on?"

"I don't have time right now."

"Meyer."

He told her to go to bed. He had one hand on the small of his back, the half-opened safe door in his other. He was tired and so he brought the Colt right out into the room, tucking it into his belt. He hitched his trousers, then secured the gun again, then he drew his coat shut by jerking both lapels.

"We're going to a dark garage in the middle of the night," he said. "You wanted an answer and I'm giving you an answer."

She stood there receding into vagueness. People you knew began to fade in this way, like angels or ghosts.

The bridge was empty and gleaming in the dark, and Ben had his pistol on the seat between them as they crossed the river into Manhattan. Pale globes lit up the steel cables and the huge pointed arches of the far tower. All he could see of Ben in the dark was his silhouette, his hat, the shoulder of his camel-hair coat.

"Jesus Christ," Ben said. "I'm in there talking about Scanlon locking himself out of the garage."

Meyer shook his head. Madison Street, Pike, Allen. Ben opened the trunk and Meyer held up the flashlight and they got their things and went into a card game in the basement of a grocer's on Rivington. Maybe he was too tired to evaluate any of this. Maybe Vito Genovese hadn't wanted to disturb him at home. He should have called.

He brought the pipe down on the dealer's wrist and Ben flailed at everyone's heads with an iron bar, the lamp swinging on its chain. Shadows flashed and tilted on the shop walls, hats aslant, the players bucking back in their folding chairs. They all went to the ground, the money scattered among the broken glass and blood. The dealer wore a seaman's cap and a shirt rolled to the elbows. He lay on his hip where the game had been, his legs slowly peddling, braying. A damp stain spread down·the inseam of his pants. Meyer planted a foot on his collarbone, then struck the wrist again where it was already broken. He could feel the scream travel up his leg, childlike and shrill. The splintered bone jabbed out through the skin in a dark smear. He held his foot in place and watched the roll and jerk, about to hit him again, not doing it, not kicking him.

He dropped the pipe and breathed. He looked Ben in the eye and Ben glared back, hamstrung, knowing it was over but not wanting it to be over. His face was handsome but distorted. He let the bar fall to the floor and told them where Vito Genovese could find them, and then they left.

"He should have called," Meyer said.

"Next time he'll call. I'll take you up to the hotel."

"We need to find Charlie."

His hands felt greasy from gripping the pipe. The baby would have all of this history now before it even came into the world. The baby would have a stunted mind. You put tiny mitts on a baby's hands so it wouldn't scratch its own face.

IV

Adhesive tape covered [Luciano's] mouth. His face and head were bruised, his eyes swollen almost shut. A knife wound had opened his right cheek, the cut stretching from his eye to his chin. There was blood on his shirt and tiny holes as if he had been pricked with an ice pick.

As Lansky bent over his friend, [Luciano] groaned and tried to open his eyes. It was difficult, but he recognized Lansky and managed a grin....

"Nobody'll believe I got taken for a ride and lived. It just ain't natural."

"You're just lucky, I guess," said Lansky....

Lucky, as everyone now called him, was quickly back on the street.

The doctor broke the news gently. Bernard, as the boy had been named before birth, was a cripple....

"It's a judgment," [Anne] screamed. "A judgment from God."

— **Hank Messick,** *Lansky*

5

Criminology

BROOKLYN, 2010

In 2010, after Gila had told me of her affair with Lansky, I took the 3 train to Brownsville, the only white person in the car until a few Hasidim got on and then off again somewhere where the tracks rose aboveground. The 24-hour deli was shut on all sides, the steel doors tagged with graffiti. Lott Avenue, Rockaway Avenue — beyond weeds and ailanthus trees stretched a vast asphalt lot, empty except for a row of electrical boxes near the chain-link fence. I took a photograph. I took another photograph of an old building with four garbage cans chained in front of it beside the Olutunu Cherubim & Seraphim Church. "Can it be saved?" asked a man in an army coat, speaking about the building or perhaps the world. On Pitkin Avenue people loitered and smoked and shopped — *Fish Sandwich, Burger, ATM* — but the side streets were almost empty, lined with row houses, a storefront church, a group of Caribbean men playing dominos on the hood of someone's car. There were once seventy Orthodox synagogues in Brownsville. There were still dairy cows in that part of Brooklyn then. My grandparents on my father's side had lived there, people I hardly knew. Number 33 Chester Street was where Meyer Lansky and his family had first lived after coming from Grodno, before they moved to the Lower East Side. All that world was gone now. Now 33 Chester Street was a vacant lot full of construction debris and weeds. Across from it was a juvenile detention facility that took up an entire block, a pink brick structure with almost no windows, concertina wire atop the high walls, catching plastic.

The destination of this journey is home. Upon arrival, we will find, as we might have expected, that home is no longer there.

Number 33 Chester Street.

All this lore I know now. All this lore because of what Gila Konig told me before she died.

6

Immigrants, Part 2

NEW YORK, 1982

Gila watched the leaves in the Park rattle on the trees or billow into the shapes of clouds when the wind shifted — elms and alders and planes. European trees, American trees. There had been whole forests of such trees outside Foehrenwald, even outside Bergen-Belsen, not that she remembered them as anything more distinct than an idea. The years of her earliest childhood had become a cubist blur of trees, leaves, frost. All that time living inside her own head — once you started that, it was difficult to stop. Budapest, Belsen, Foehrenwald, Tel Aviv. Now it was 1982. Her first week in New York, almost two years ago now, she had walked down Seventh Avenue and seen the garment district — mannequins in tiny plexiglass displays, steam rising from the manholes, hand trucks and aluminum racks crammed with parkas. She'd looked at the crowd and could imagine no way in.

Some students still lingered in the dim hallway when she came back inside. They were boys in expensive sports clothes with awkward wavy hair, the first fringes of mustache on some of their lips, aware, she guessed, of what had just happened in class. She greeted them — *Mah ha'inyanim* — and they looked at her and gave their rote answer, then went back to jeering about subjects she knew nothing about, from TV. She went into the bathroom and washed her face, preparing for what was next, then dried off with paper towels and glimpsed herself in the mirror — pale skin, no makeup, black hair pulled back, a few strands trailing into green eyes. She was forty-three, a Hebrew teacher. The bathroom walls behind her were the grayish pink of old hospitals. The temple had once been a movie theater, Rabbi Lehman had told her. Plastic dispensers leaked thin yellow soap onto the stainless-steel counter.

She walked down the hall to Lehman's office. What she guessed from the solemn look on his face was that he was going to draw this out into a mournful discussion in which her only possible role could be that of noble survivor. She stood there behind the empty chair and Lehman rubbed the corner of his tired eye with a fully extended index finger. He had taken off the jacket of his three-piece suit but the vest was still on. He nodded slowly, his head turned, his hand lightly caressing his beard.

"You know what it's like by now," he said, still not looking at her. "The ignorance. Whatever you want to call it. This country. Our shame. Our *schande*."

"I lost my temper," she said. "It was not a big deal."

"Robby Karsh will apologize. You'll apologize to Robby Karsh." He put his hand dyspeptically over his ribs, wincing a little. "As a gesture. As a start."

"He doesn't have to apologize."

"He's an obnoxious kid. But he's also just a twelve-year-old."

The textbook sat on Lehman's desk. On its cover was a blue

cartoon dragon that spoke Hebrew. It had been defaced by Robby Karsh, who had drawn a swastika on the creature's forehead. Before that, the dragon had been a figure grubby and feisty enough for the students to have embraced without question or doubt. For the past two weeks, they had all been learning Hebrew in relative calm.

"You shouldn't have slapped him," Lehman said. "That of course is what changes it into Max Stone teaching your classes next week."

She turned, then consciously readjusted her hands on her thigh. She looked back down at him. "He can keep the classes," she said.

"Gila."

"He can keep the Nazis too. The Shoah. The holiness of it. He likes to talk about it more than I do."

Lehman drew in a beseeching breath, as if his sympathy for her anger was fraught with risk. "Can't we have this talk later?"

"I think we've already had it."

She came back to find the girl, Hannah, waiting for her alone in the classroom. The desks were disarranged on the gray floor and there were still fragments of Hebrew letters on the blackboard, yellow flecks missed by the eraser. Gila retrieved her purse from behind the desk and the girl looked up from her Walkman, which she was tinkering with rather than listening to. Her dark hair hung in loose curls and she wore one of her father's old dress shirts, far too large, frayed at the collar and cuffs. She appeared to be still upset — not shocked, but offended — by Gila's outburst. It must have seemed unprovoked, slightly deranged, aimed not just at Robby Karsh but at the class in general. It must have seemed that way because that was how it had felt to Gila herself. But it had been Hannah's fault.

"Are you ready?" Gila asked.

Hannah shrugged.

"Where's your bag?"

"It's in the coatroom," Hannah said. "Where it always is. No one's going to steal it."

"You could have picked it up."

"I'll get it on the way out."

Gila looked at the floor. "You told my story to Robby Karsh," she said. "You must have told it to him at some point."

Hannah's eyes went a little narrow, a kind of thoughtful squint that often masked her actual thoughtlessness. She had the naïve brown eyes of a dog, a narrow face like something carved out of sandalwood.

"I guess Robby Karsh thought it was funny," Gila said. "I thought you understood why I told you that story."

The girl kept meeting her gaze with that odd thoughtful poise. Gila could see now that Hannah didn't know why she'd repeated the story to Robby Karsh. All she knew — or sensed, gradually — was that she'd done something a little obscene, which, to Gila, seemed the inevitable result of telling such stories.

What they'd subsisted on in Bergen-Belsen, she'd told Hannah, was a watery broth made of boiled nettles — nettles, she'd explained, were a kind of weed whose leaves were said to taste somewhat like artichokes. She'd never been able to eat an artichoke, she'd told Hannah. She and her mother had had one bowl of the nettle soup to split between them each day. It was at the very end of the war, a season of typhus, overcrowding, a near total breakdown of logistics (there were no tattoos, she'd explained, not all the camps did that anyway). Her mother didn't share the soup with the dozens of other starving women and children in their barracks, with the thousands of other starving women and children outside the barracks. To share would have been to jeopardize their own lives. Of course there was more to the story, such as how her mother had gotten the bowl of soup in the first place. Where her mother had gone when Gila waited in the little room outside the vestibule of the infirmary. What her mother had done to keep them alive. That part of the story she had not shared with Hannah.

They walked up 79th Street, not talking, Hannah listening to the tape player now, her duffel bag over her shoulder. Gila carried a small suitcase for their trip to the country with Hannah's father. His store filled two high stories of a white-brick building, its windows bordered in gold, each window shaded by a monogrammed green canopy embossed with a gold letter G. Inside, pale carpets caught the light from outside and made the shop half drawing room, half museum — a Chinese horse of brown and green enamel, across the room a marble statue of Apollo. Upstairs, among the English and French furniture, a few gowns hung before tall mirrors and within the opened doors of armoires.

He was a large white-haired man in an olive-colored suit. He breathed in, as if annoyed, then said hello and Hannah turned off her Walkman.

"I need a different coat," she said. "Everyone wears these coats now."

"We'll buy you a new wardrobe."

"I don't want a new wardrobe, I want a different coat."

"Fiorucci. Maybe you'd like that."

It was impossible to know if he was joking or serious. Gila stood there with her suitcase on the floor beside her, not so much as spectator but as attendant. They were fighting — this was the way they fought. Her presence here was the opposite of the Hebrew lessons, where every kind of gaze assailed her from every angle at all times. It should have been easy enough to adjust from one role to the other — visible there, not here — but the basic trick still eluded her.

They walked down to the dim garage with its office and punch clock, prices in black on the huge white sign. Groff waited for them to get into the car. The Lincoln had power locks and a leather strap you used to pull the heavy door shut. They drove down York Avenue to Sutton Place, then took 57th Street to the turnoff onto the Queensboro Bridge, Gila in back, Hannah up front beside her father, Groff staring stoically at the traffic, Gila looking into Hannah's side mirror at the reflected skyline.

His wife had been in a restaurant nine months ago when she'd gone into a seizure and fallen out of her chair. That was how all this had started — the babysitting for someone who didn't really need a babysitter, the twelve-year-old girl whose mother was in and out of the hospital until one night she wasn't. On one of those nights when Gila was alone with the terrified girl, the TV lights flashing on the walls of her bedroom, Hannah curled on the floor with a quilted blanket, not crying but frustrated, angry, Gila had told her the story of the camps and the nettle soup. You had to be strong in the face of enormous sadness. That was the simple point of the story. But perhaps the point was simply overwhelming. She had never had children of her own. Perhaps it was no wonder if she did all the wrong things with Hannah.

*   *   *

The house was on a large pond north of the village, a mile from the bay, two and a half miles from the ocean. It had sat empty all that spring and all that summer, even when there was no longer any reason to remain away, even after Groff's wife, Mona, had died. The headlights shone on the front windows where the roses had sprawled in thin, mad tentacles. When Groff switched on the porch lights, the moths came fluttering around. He'd asked Gila to come along on this first trip because he couldn't face it, he said. He said he'd talked to Hannah about it and Hannah wanted her to come too. He was frequently candid in this way, in short bursts. It wasn't that he spoke the language of charm, it was that he somehow embodied charm in all its subtle confusion. His ugliness was charming. His silence was charming. His apparent repudiation of all things charming was part of his charm.

Hannah went up to her bedroom and Groff went back to town to get some dinner, so Gila set the table. The kitchen smelled intoxicatingly of mold. Wood everywhere — varnished floors and exposed beams on the ceiling and the wood of the staircase, the dark frames of the windows. She saw his wife's taste in dishes — festive bright plates, yellow or orange. Dingy, cheap silverware, amber-colored glasses. The moldy scent and the scent of lemon floor wax gave Gila a feeling not unlike déjà vu, only there were no memories attached to it. Dried flowers in a vase. A kind of potent nostalgia for a place she'd never been, a home she'd never had.

————————

There was an old poster on the wall of Hannah's bedroom — she'd forgotten it until she went in, planning to call her friend, but when she saw it she put on her Walkman and sat on the bed, hunched there in her salvaged clothes, her father's baggy dress shirt. There was the small black-and-white TV, the Woody Woodpecker doll, the pink-and-blue desk with its matching chair. There was her mother's eager, ironic smile looking down on it all, all those toys and games she had bought for Hannah, both laughing at them and with them, as if she'd had a hand in inventing them herself. The poster on the wall showed a disco group in an exuberant Broadway tableau above a set of piano keys that matched the starry midnight sky behind them. The word "camp" had more than one meaning, Hannah's mother had explained once, one of those meanings being "playful" — the poster and the disco group it portrayed were very "camp," her mother had said. Hannah listened to the song on her Walkman and saw a blue-and-green swirl like the ocean viewed from a distant height. A new kind of song, mechanistic and cold, the drum machine's synthetic hand claps coming with such concussive force that they seemed to assert a kind of meaning, like code from some other, more allusive world.

Mr. Stone, the older Hebrew teacher, was always giving his condolences about her mother, and he would sometimes ask her about Gila too. He was a sullen man with an old-fashioned Bronx accent and synthetic dress slacks, age spots on his hands. He knew the whole story — the babysitting last spring during the hospital stays, then her mother's death. It's not that bad, Hannah had wanted to say. But of course that isn't what she'd said. Her contempt for Stone was not pure, it was laced with awkwardness. What she'd said was: *Did Gila ever tell you about the camps?*

You told my story to Robby Karsh. I thought you understood why I told you that story.

It was such a strange, impersonal accusation, to think Hannah would have told that story to a boy like Robby Karsh, to any of those boys. It meant that Gila didn't know anything about her, that she understood Hannah as nothing more than another student in that lifeless, spoiled class. The accusation had surprised her so much she hadn't even been able to deny it. But maybe she wasn't so different from the other students after all. Why else had she told the story to Mr. Stone? Out of awkwardness. Out of embarrassment. She had told the story to Mr. Stone just to make him stop talking.

As for Robby Karsh, he had no idea about Gila. He'd just drawn the swastika as a joke.

———

Pizza in the white box, the salad already wilting in its foil tray. The room was too quiet so Groff put on the radio. The receiver glowed an efficient yellow beneath the dial, the nearby college station playing jazz.

"I have to go out a little later," he said.

Hannah looked up from her plate. Groff turned his hand palm up.

"You have a big date?" Hannah said.

"That isn't funny."

"If you're just going to the Kleins', why can't I come?"

"It's late. It's already late."

Gila was hardly listening. She was thinking things through. For example, neither Groff nor Hannah knew she had quit her job at the temple that afternoon. She thought of Hannah's face in the classroom — that poise, older than Hannah's age — and wondered how much Hannah suspected.

Groff looked at her, his eyes seeing her but also denying everything about her that wasn't relevant to this particular moment. "I won't be long," he said. "There's a movie player — Hannah can show you how it works. I don't know what there is — old tennis matches — Wimbledon. You won't want to watch that, but there are movies. Hannah will show you."

He bit into the crust of his pizza, hungrily chewing. The way he ate was so unself-conscious that the room became calmer.

———

A desk, a bed, a mat on the floor, a dresser with broken handles so that she left the drawers partly opened — this was how Gila lived in Manhattan now. Outside, the city withered, food wrappers and empty cans in an abandoned station wagon, the local shop displaying soap and toothpaste. Her building belonged to a congregant at the temple, that was why the rent was low. She could hear other people's TVs in the airshaft as she tried to sleep. At first, she'd felt obliged to go to services, sitting there before the cantor's modal gloom, the loud seconding of the organ, Rabbi Lehman circulating the undressed Torah to the nearly empty pews. They treated her like some sort of wraith, someone foreign to have opinions about.

Not long after he'd hired her, Groff had given her a gift from his shop that hung on the wall of her apartment now, a framed poster from the 1930s, the glass cloudy, the image a hazy black and white. At the bottom was the name Elsa Schiaparelli, the designer, who was posed in profile, her hands clasped casually over the arm of a gilt chair, black hair knotted at one side, a white gown falling off one shoulder in a cowl of fabric cut like feathers. At the top, in pink letters, was the single word *Shocking!* She had mentioned to him once that she'd wanted to be a designer. He'd remembered.

"It must be worth something," she said.

"Not really," he answered. "Not much. These things just accumulate. Don't take it if you don't like it."

He was still holding it against his hip.

"I used to make drawings," she said. "Schiaparelli. Chanel. I used to dream about those things, even when I was a little girl. Even when I was younger than Hannah."

He put the poster down on the counter and looked at her. He seemed on the verge of probing for more, then she could see him decide not to.

"Fine, good," he said. "Then it's yours."

———

He came back a little after ten, moving in the lamplight with a tight chest, not looking too much at anything. Mona's things, his things — the Turkish rug, rose colored, the worn sofas, the end tables with their stacks of magazines. The sunroom lay beyond it, its windows on the pond a lustrous black. In the kitchen, he found an old bottle of rum and poured some into a glass with some ice, the Haitian kind he liked, Barbancourt. He wished he could have stayed at the Kleins', the candles burning over the two different hearths, the women in their sweaters and jeans and high boots, food all around, the different wines. Harry Klein sold commercial real estate. He did impressions and told obscene jokes, even racist jokes, and he read *Anna Karenina* every year. Mona had liked to help him prune the fruit trees on the side of his property each March, standing on the ladder with her long streaked hair blowing in her eyes, her rag wool gloves.

She'd been a photographer, known in a modest way for portraits of criminals in the documentary style of Robert Frank. In the city's interrogation rooms, the police would set up a clock beside their suspects to serve as a time marker during their video-taped statements. Mona's photographs showed these suspects, black or Hispanic usually, listless or defiant or in tears, always with that clock in the frame, its pointing hands.

Metastasis — the liver, the lungs, even the brain. There was the wait while they hydrated her, the wait while they ran the bloodwork, the wait while they brought her to the chair and ran the chemo, the wait in the office. *People* magazine, *Car and Driver, Highlights*. The wait in the bedroom while she prepared herself to come back out after a bath, her hair gone, even her eye-brows, her face somehow naked, scalded. One time he'd asked her how she felt and she'd said, "I'm scared," and it was like the only honest thing he'd ever heard. There was nothing that could pre-pare you for how it felt, the tubes in her bruised arm, the EKG, the paper gown, Mona so emaciated she seemed half her size, as if she wasn't anyone in particular anymore, or as if the machines were there for the simple purpose of stealing her identity.

He switched off the lamp and stood for a while in the living room. Hours would pass, he wouldn't sleep, he knew it already. The furnace ticked erratically in the walls, then came on with a low muffled whoosh. The loss felt more like fear now. It came at him backwards. What he feared had already happened. When he turned off the light in the hallway, the darkness was a thickness, a presence in the air. He opened his eyes and it was no different from having them closed. The city was never dark in that way. It was a darkness you breathed.

He switched the light back on and saw the bedroom down the hall where Gila was. His resolve rose and then waned in a way that was dizzying — he imagined it happening and then it happened. It had happened before. He went ahead and approached her door absently, his fingers resting for a moment on the glass knob. He paused as if about to knock, then thought about the noise and instead he slowly opened it, stepping forward like a wary child. She turned in bed with an intake of breath. She had fallen asleep with a magazine on the blanket beside her. The smell of her sleep filled the room. It was impossible to do this with any grace.

"I still have a few things to learn," he said.

She rubbed her eyes, then switched on the bedside lamp. "Like what?" she said.

"Lots of things. How to live without scruples."

She turned away and he moved farther into the room, sitting in a little chair by the door in his overcoat.

"I quit my job," she said.

"When?"

"This afternoon. I can't do it anymore. It was time."

She wanted to open a store — women's clothes, evening wear. He had promised once he would help her. This was what she was really saying.

"I was hoping Hannah would learn Hebrew," he said, his eyes closed. "They teach her French in school — nice, fine — but what does it really have to do with anything, French?"

"It's a nice house you have. A nice life."

"This was the room she fussed over. The guest room. I never understood why. People coming to visit. Endless."

He brought his hand back to his shoulder and massaged it. She was looking at the magazine now, one of Mona's, *Aperture*. The lamp, the window valances, the sleigh bed from the shop in East Hampton.

"I thought we'd go on the boat tomorrow with the Kleins," he said.

"You go."

"You'll stay here and read my wife's magazines."

"I don't like boats. I also don't like playing games."

"Of course you do."

He stood up and finished the drink, the warmth filling his chest.

"Just stay," she said. "I'm sorry. I'm being crazy."

"Not crazy."

"Crazy. I can see that."

The lamp threw its garish cone of light on her side of the room, exposing the tangled pattern of the Victorian wallpaper. Mona's *Aperture*. That world she'd wanted to enter, its soundless black-and-white stillness. He watched his hand to steady it as he bent down to put his glass on the floor beside the chair. He tried to move more slowly. She reached her hand out toward him and let it rest on the blanket. He lay on the bed beside her with his coat still on, his shoes. A lot like Mona and nothing at all like Mona. He kissed her neck just below the ear and she rolled toward him and he felt her bare waist beneath the T-shirt, the warmth of her skin, the curve of her breasts.

———————

In the temple, on the walls of the hallway leading back to the classrooms, Mr. Stone had erected a kind of shrine: black-and-white photographs of decimated men in rags, shaven-headed men naked in piles, dead bodies in the open pit — Auschwitz, Treblinka, Bergen-Belsen — he would intone the names in the mournful lilt of prayer. The ones who weren't naked wore clownish striped suits and caps, the teeth falling out of their skulls. Mr. Stone wanted you not to understand but to feel complicit. He wanted you to be answerable for a catastrophe so distant you could only resent him for presenting it to you, those withered people behind the barbed-wire fence.

That first night Gila had come to the apartment, she'd hardly spoken to Hannah, even though they'd seen each other all those days at Hebrew school. Gila had had her hair not tied back but down, and she wore a black T-shirt and jeans — it occurred to Hannah for the first time that Gila had a private life she knew nothing about. Her clothes, her loose hair cut straight just above her shoulders, not tied back or pinned, faint lines at the edges of her green eyes, but her clothes the clothes of a young person — the shock of the way she looked, that and her coldness, her silence. She read a fashion magazine while Hannah watched TV. Maybe Hannah had fallen a little in love with her over the course of those nights. Maybe that was why she'd told Mr. Stone her story of the camps.

It was sunny the next morning and she and her father went to the nature preserve on Noyac Road, a place they always went. They could see cardinals in the thicket as they walked toward the bay. He was telling her that Gila had quit her job at the temple. It was something she'd wanted to do for a long time.

"We're fond of each other," he said then. "Maybe you already know that. I don't know. I just wanted to tell you. I don't expect you to be happy about it or to understand it, but I wanted to tell you. I tell you everything. That's the rule."

The leaves shone against the clear blue sky, a preposterous display — tupelo, oak — the colors throbbing faintly, they were so bright. She knew the names of the trees because her mother had taught them to her. Her mother had bought her the coat she was wearing, dark olive, the waxed cotton shiny like oilcloth, the kind of preppy jacket all the girls wore except the kind of girl she wanted to be now.

"I'm sorry," her father said. "I'm sorry if this makes it worse. It was already the worst."

It was when he touched her arm that she fully understood. It was like he was holding his hands over her face. She found herself clenching in spasm. All these things at once now: the embarrassment of her crying, the violence of it, the nausea quivering down her throat. Far ahead of them, a girl stood near the bushes, extending her hand, trying to get birds to eat seeds out of her open palm. The bushes were called catbrier. Catbrier, tupelo, oak. She didn't know why she was crying. She scratched at her face but she didn't feel anything but the sun glare. She pushed her father away and started running, as if there were anyplace to run.

She watched from the car as he carried Gila's bag and they went into her building through the glass door. It was a squat red box, dwarfed by the white-brick complex that filled up the rest of the block all the way to York. There was a sign that said H. KOTZ MEDICAL SUPPLIES and beside it SYLVIE'S EUROPEAN ALTERATIONS, the signs so old they looked not like advertisements but commemorations. It was just blocks from where she lived, but the street was like a remnant of another world. It was the world of the temple, the world of Mr. Stone.

There would be Hebrew school next week, but Gila would not be there to teach it. Perhaps she would be here, in the squat red box, drinking tea in the dim rooms. To imagine this lonely picture was somehow to feel it as Hannah's own fault, though it hadn't even happened. She had run off into the woods crying like any other twelve-year-old girl.

The sun was hitting everything at a twilight slant when she finally got out of the car. She looked up at the building's windows — she didn't know which one was Gila's — and at the empty black lattice of the fire escape. Some men were unloading furniture from an orange truck, black men in wool caps and sweatshirts and gloves, even though it wasn't cold. Then she saw some movement behind the inner door of Gila's building and she came closer. It was an old woman looking fiercely out, a bandage behind one lens of her glasses. She started shouting inaudibly through the door. Perhaps she was mistaking Hannah for someone else.

It was a long time before her father came back downstairs. He wore a beige wool overcoat, the strands of his white hair slicked back and revealing the bald skin beneath. There was that moment before he noticed her watching, a moment of such self-containment and strength that she never wanted him to turn — she wanted to disappear, if that's what was required. Then he turned and looked at her without sympathy, as if they had suddenly become equals now. *You told my story to Robby Karsh. I thought you understood why I told you that story.* It was the last time they saw Gila together.

Part Two

In the Presence of My Enemies

7

To Israel, 2009

What we need is a memoir without a self.
A memoir about someone other than "me."

Of course I can't know what Gila and my father said or what they meant to each other almost thirty years ago, only what they came to mean to me as I imagined these scenes. While I imagined these scenes, what Gila and my father meant to each other meant more to me than I would have ever suspected. Twenty-eight years after it happened, I got a letter from Gila, who'd seen an essay I'd written about a murder in Israel, a Mafia-style murder. She wanted to tell me some things about her life in Tel Aviv, she said. It had been a long time — long enough, she hoped, that we could talk.

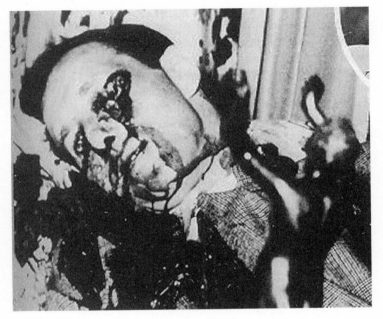

Benjamin Siegel

Meyer Lansky

I PITY THE POOR IMMIGRANT

A woman goes on a journey — Jerusalem, Bethlehem, Tel Aviv, then back to New York. I thought I was covering the murder of an Israeli poet named David Bellen, investigating a fairly straightforward crime story. But it became a story that led elsewhere, a story that led everywhere, a story I would have had no interest in if I hadn't accidentally found myself inside it. I remember standing that first night in the narcotic gray light of the terminal at JFK, its vast glowing dome momentous and boring at the same time, like some disappointing portal to an afterlife of crowds. The women in their African robes, the men in soccer jerseys, the women from Jamaica with their bright suitcases — everyone seemed suspended in that gray light. Your name is Hannah, the El Al screeners said, a Hebrew name. They asked, more than once, "Why have you never been to Israel?"

8

Kid Bethlehem:

An Investigation into the Murder of David Bellen

by Hannah Groff

> "We don't choose our obsessions — our obses-
> sions, invariably against our deepest wishes,
> choose us. Against our deepest wishes, we
> become suddenly, inexplicably committed to a
> path we had avoided, a line of thought we'd had
> no interest in."
>
> **— David Bellen, 2008**

1) GANGSTER STYLE

They found the poet David Bellen's body on the morning of
December 23, 2008, in a village called Beit Sahour, just outside Bethlehem, six miles from Jerusalem, about thirty-

seven miles from Bellen's home in Tel Aviv. As unlikely as it seemed, it was not a random place to find his body. Like other parts of the West Bank, Bethlehem has faced a growing and strategic expansion of Jewish settlements in recent years — provocation in a region rife with provocation. The city is also the setting for some of the poems in Bellen's 2008 book, *Kid Bethlehem,* which is in many ways a critique of current Israeli policy in the Occupied Territories.

A preliminary statement by the Israeli Defense Forces described the murder as most likely an act of terrorism. As it happened, they were preoccupied at the time with larger matters — Hamas, the Islamist group that controls Gaza, on the other side of Israel from the West Bank, had just terminated a cease-fire agreement five days before. The day after Bellen's murder, Hamas launched a series of mortar and rocket attacks on Israeli cities which set the stage for Israel's retaliatory air strikes of December 27. Another war had begun, code-named Operation Cast Lead — the Gaza War. In the ensuing onslaught — F-16 fighter jets, AH-64 Apache helicopters, the white and gray plumes of smoke rising like ghostly fireworks over demolished buildings — Israel and the world at large almost inevitably lost sight of the story of David Bellen's murder. As of this writing, the IDF says they are still looking for suspects. But even a basic question such as how someone like Bellen could have gotten from Tel Aviv to the Palestinian city of Bethlehem — how and why he could have possibly made such a journey, dead or alive — remains unanswered.[1]

---

1. Israeli citizens are legally barred from entering major West Bank cities such as Bethlehem due to the security risk.

2) OUR OBSESSIONS CHOOSE US

Rock stars, serial killers, drug addicts, sexual "deviants" — these are some of the obsessives that have come to obsess me in my career as a journalist. I'm not a political writer — whatever politics I've engaged in has always been far beneath the surface. I'm a crime writer with a fractured style. I pitched this story as a crime story.

But when I left for Israel, I felt as though it were the 1980s and I was telling friends I wanted to visit South Africa. What I would say now, having gone, is that if Israel were to disappear, my friends might be the very people who would erect a sentimental cult in its memory. I had never cared much about Israel — my lack of interest was so long-standing that perhaps I should have wondered more about it. On a deeper level, I might have realized, I had never wanted to face too directly the idea of myself as a Jew. Your name is Hannah, the El Al people kept pointing out to me in the security line, a Hebrew name — why had I never been to Israel? They were smiling as they said it, but it was precisely this kind of righteous shaming that I have always taken pains to avoid.

My favorite picture of David Bellen, who disliked having his photograph taken, is badly focused and in black-and-white. He has a squat bald head and wears metal-rimmed, Soviet-looking glasses. He looks like a wry pugilist, used to taking blows to the face. Inspired by the paintings of an Israeli artist named Ivan Schwebel, he wrote his last book, *Kid Bethlehem,* in his midsixties, in the years leading up to the Gaza War — years of disillusionment, cynicism, terror, and other wars, in which Israel became more than ever in the world's eyes an oppressor, a kind of gangster state. The poems in Bellen's book, like Schwebel's paintings, are a peculiar retelling of the story of King David — his rise, his triumph, his decadence, his tragedy, his death. As in Schwebel's paintings, Bellen's David appears in modern guise — particularly, in Bellen's poems, in the counterpersona of the real-life Israeli gangster Yehezkel Aslan, who died in 1993. Because of the book's controversial nature, it can't help but be looked at as a clue to Bellen's murder.

3) THE ROUTE

You could take one fork of the Hebron Road all the way from Jerusalem to Bethlehem, my driver explained, but it would mean going through the main checkpoint, which could add as much as an hour to the tiny six-mile trip, so instead we went the circuitous way along Route 60 to the West Bank town of Beit Jala. It was the first time I'd seen the separation wall, high barriers made of wood or maybe some bulletproof polymer that looked like wood. We passed through a tunnel that seemed like any other tunnel until we emerged from it and there it was — vast, brutal, brown — lining the road on one side like an endless fan whose blades had been bent in half, the top half casting a shadow. Spread over the valley beyond were houses of white stone and pink tile, cypress trees, grass. On one hillside was a dilapidated Arab settlement. On the opposite hillside was a shiny Jewish one. My driver had a tired air, as if he saw himself as a kind of character. He shrugged and pointed out the large gaps in the wall that anyone who wanted to could walk right through. Thousands of shooting incidents until they built the wall between Gilo and Beit Jala, he said. Sometimes the Arabs would open fire on the highway traffic, sometimes they would shoot across the valley at the Jewish settlements, sometimes the Jews would shoot back. I mentioned nothing about David Bellen. I think the reason I didn't was that I was afraid the driver would not have heard of him.

We parked in front of a convenience store in Beit Jala and I waited to change to a Palestinian driver. Dust, construction, a checkpoint with a single black-and-white car with the flag of the Palestinian Authority. The storekeeper offered me a bottle of water, and then a group of tourists came in an SUV and we all got into the new driver's van. When his cell phone rang, it played "Careless Whisper." As we drove on toward Bethlehem, he said, "I will tell you this little story and at the end you will be amused."

He pulled over on the embankment in Beit Sahour as I'd requested and pointed out the site I'd asked to see, the Shepherds' Field, the place where the biblical David is said to have grazed his sheep. The hillsides were covered with the concrete slabs of half-built houses, cypress trees, rocks. I took a few photographs. We weren't allowed to go down any closer, the driver said, because it was dangerous. He meant it was always dangerous. He wasn't saying that this was the place, six months before, where the IDF had found David Bellen's mutilated body in a vacant lot among the building sites. I tried to picture it there — I knew the body had been run over by a truck sev-

The crime scene, Beit Sahour, on the eastern edge of Bethlehem

eral times, most likely to make it harder to determine the precise cause of death. It was as if the battered corpse was left there as a message: *Not there, but here. Not in Tel Aviv, but in Bethlehem. Not in the modern city, but in the birthplace of the ancient king.*

4) TURF WAR

At first I found it frustrating that the politics of ancient Israel were confusing to me in exactly the same way as the politics of modern Israel, frustrating that I had such a poor grasp of either. At the time of David, the twelve tribes, themselves grouped into factions — Israel and Judah — were surrounded by enemies that included the Philistines, the Amalekites, the Ammonites, and the

Phoenicians. It was hard for me to keep track of these names, hard because they didn't concern me personally. It was hard for me to keep track of Iran, Syria, Lebanon, Fatah, Hamas, Hezbollah, Islamic Jihad, the al-Aqsa Martyrs Brigades, etc. As a journalist, my job was to make all this transparent. Instead, I often felt less knowledgeable than the reader I was supposed to be informing.

11 Jerusalem Arab teens arrested yesterday for desecrating Jewish graves on the Mount of Olives, I read in the *Jerusalem Post* on my second morning in Israel. I looked out at the cemetery from my hotel room in the German Colony south of Mount Zion. Still jet-lagged, I saw the Dome of the Rock shining bronze at dawn.

5) THE MYSTERY DEEPENS

The next day, I met with the journalist Oded Voss at a café across the street from the King David Hotel. Voss, a veteran of the First Lebanon War, is handsome, intelligent, with skeptical blue eyes and gray flecks in his neat beard and precisely cut hair. Over lunch, he recounted for me his efforts to cover the Bellen murder until the lack of new information — and the lack of public inter-est — caused him to stop. He said that the idea of Bellen leaving Tel Aviv on his own for an illegal nighttime journey to the West Bank made no sense to anyone. What did make sense was the killers leaving his body in the symbolic place that they did. "But the reason could be simple or complicated," he went on. He started to elaborate, meeting my eyes, but seemed defeated by the effort.

"At least one of my fears has not materialized," he said. "After six months, at least we don't have a Palestinian sitting in jail for it."

I asked why a Palestinian would want to murder someone like David Bellen. "In a sense, that's right," Voss said.

"Then what I'm asking is why the IDF would call it an act of terrorism."

He looked at me before answering this. Later, I realized that during this moment he was parsing my naïveté, assessing its precise components.

"Jews are murdered here all the time," he said. "The world doesn't really like to remember that, but that might be why the IDF said what it said."

He looked away as if scanning the traffic, his hands and forearms resting on the table. What I felt then was different from the mild shaming I'd felt from the El Al screeners at the airport. Until I got my bearings, I felt that I could not do this story, that I was not equipped for it, intellectually or otherwise. I went over the various scenarios. That Bellen had been murdered by extremist Jews who hated his book's sacrilegious treatment of the David story. That he had been murdered by Palestinians, perhaps simply at random, perhaps because of his relative notoriety. Both scenarios seemed unlikely. There was another theory, only hinted at, that I'd found in an interview given by Bellen's editor, Galit Levy. Levy declared that the murder could not be understood without answering the simple question of how someone could be run over by a truck as many as twelve times in a densely populated district like Beit Sahour without attracting any witnesses. I assumed she was implying the presence in Beit Sahour of a militia group or some type of organized crime.

"Those are some of the possibilities people come up with," Voss said when I asked his opinion.

"But no one believes them."

He shrugged one shoulder and let out a disgusted breath. "Believe. Not believe. What are the facts?"

6) NOT FUNNY

Around this time, I happened to watch the Pacino remake of *Scarface.* It's not a good movie. It's a bad movie, but it resonates — it resonates all across the globe. And I thought, why am I so bored with poetry? In the movie, once Tony Montana kills his way to the top, he has not even one second of happiness. A montage set to cheap music, then it's coke addiction, bad sex, doom. I thought, that's David, his whole rise and fall. That's it.

— **David Bellen, 2008**

In America, Jewish writers are frequently, sometimes compulsively, funny. The writing of David Bellen started to make me think this was problematic. *Kid Bethlehem* is a cubist jumble of short numbered sections. In addition to poems, there are quotations, scraps of memoir, reportage, scripture, newspaper clippings. The book, particularly in light of Bellen's violent death, has made the world look even more fragmented to me now, more disjointed, shattered by some profound if intangible trauma. I have found myself imitating its form and tone in this essay you're reading now.

Kid Bethlehem

*Trouble from the minute he left his sheep
and that rocky place
threatened by the lion and the bear
to soothe King Saul with his harp,
then kill Goliath with a small hard stone*

*A stone killer —
it was all the women talked about, so Saul
needed him hit
The war advanced on all fronts
Who knows
why any of this had to happen?*

*Warsaw, Lodz, Auschwitz, Babi Yar,
Murder Inc., Beirut
The rockets arcing toward Tel Aviv
As in days of old
before
the coming of
the King David Hotel*

*They said God was dead, but God is not
God is the small hard stone
in the boy's sling*

7) THE VALLEY OF ELAH

After our lunch that day, Voss went with me on what I thought might be a fool's errand: one of my guidebooks indicated that somewhere near the junction of Route 38 and Route 383 was a hill, or *tel*, called Azeka, which looked down on the Valley of Elah, where David had killed Goliath.

We drove once again along the separation wall — Jewish settlements on one hillside, Arab settlements on the opposite ones, just as three thousand years ago it had been Israelites and Philistines. It was such an obvious parallel that I was embarrassed even to be thinking about it, sitting next to Voss in the Mercedes taxi. He wore a dark blue shirt, unbuttoned at the neck, and a black suit. While we drove, he solemnly checked his BlackBerry and made a few phone calls in Hebrew, a language I can read phonetically but I don't speak.

Far outside Jerusalem, we entered a region of large farms and pine-covered mountains. The clouds thickened until the hillsides, with their undulating smooth stones and sparse bushes, looked uncannily biblical. We were lost. The driver pulled over and he and Voss had a conversation in Hebrew while they looked at the driver's enormous folding map. I finally suggested that we ask the boy who was waiting at a rural bus stop just up the road. We drove there. The boy turned out to be a recent immigrant from Manchester, England. He wore surfer's shorts and a white button-down shirt and a skullcap of multicolored yarn. I explained in English what we were trying to find, and he knew exactly what I was talking about. He leaned in the window and gave Voss and the driver precise directions in Hebrew.

"Lots of Brits coming into this area," Voss grunted. "More true believers. Another wave."

The road dead-ended at the top of the hill, so Voss and I got out of the car and continued up on foot. It was a steep rocky path and when I slipped a little, looking down at my camera, Voss caught me lightly by the arm. He did this out of simple instinct, but he was a little ceremonious about making sure I'd regained my balance. He was handsome and everything about his movements was imbued with the habits of handsomeness.

"A beautiful view," he said at the top of the hill. "I guess you'll expense the ride."

"Not likely. Not for a story about a dead Israeli poet."

The dry grass and weeds below us — gold, gray, brown, mustard — began to blaze up in their colors as the sun emerged through the clouds. I pictured the boy David running out in sandals, arms stabbing the air, a slingshot in his hand.

"It could have been a suicide," Voss said. "Bellen's death. That's what I sometimes think."

8) CITADEL

My first glimpse of the Old City of Jerusalem came after a picturesque climb up the western slope on a dirt path through pines and flowering shrubs. I took a chance right turn into the fortified wall and found myself in a silent alley of stone — stone steps, stone walls, all of it swelling with a gold light unlike anything I'd ever seen. The sky above it was cloudless and thickly blue. Because there were no people there — because it happened to be empty — the alley appeared timeless, the stairway a mystical symbol. I walked up the alley to the Zion Gate into an exotic place far more beautiful and seductive than I had expected. I had to come to terms with the powerful fact that Israel is physically beautiful. The name is beautiful — not just the sound, which is sonorous, but the meaning: "one who wrestles with God." The idea of a people naming themselves that way is beautiful. I had to try hard not to be seduced. The stairs and the fortified walls were replicas of stairs and fortified walls from hundreds of years ago. The city itself was thousands of years older than those earlier stairs and fortified walls. When David first conquered Jerusalem and established his capital there, it had belonged to a forgotten people called the Jebusites, about whom we know nothing. I had to remember that the people who lived there now were as distant from the people who had built the original city as I was.

9) THE VIEW FROM THE HILL

A suicide. I tried to think my way through this statement as we stood there on top of Tel Azeka. The more I thought about it the more it seemed that Voss was making some kind of absurdist joke. We were walking down the other side of the hill now toward the dry creek bed near the highway, the creek bed where three thousand years ago David had chosen the stone for his slingshot. Everything below was green and beige — the farm fields in the valley, the pines and the cedars — but the landscape was fixed in the present by the road and the industrial-style planting of the crops. Voss began to elaborate, after I prodded him. Imagine you were sixty-five years old, he said, with a history of depression and your life's work once again about to reveal itself as virtually irrelevant. The cease-fire with Hamas had just ended, the Gaza War was imminent, your most recent book of poems — a prize-winning book you had spent five years writing — had sold just a thousand copies, received a mixture of respectful and hostile reviews, and within a few months was all but forgotten except by some fanatics who hadn't actually read it. He said that he himself had experienced severe depressions in the past, periods of weeks or even months when the pointlessness of his work, or a guilty memory, or the sense that the world was winding down — all these forms of despair that sound so frivolous when you're on the other side of them — became constant and fixed. He would see very clearly how little difference it made if he lived or died. In that disturbed state of mind, the only thing that kept Voss from killing himself, he said, was the thought of his family and friends, and how much it would sadden them. He said that if he'd been able to imagine a way to disguise the suicide as an accident or a murder, we might not be taking this walk right now.

He was squinting a little in the sunlight — it struck me as notable somehow that he wasn't wearing sunglasses. He walked with his hands held near his chest, slowly massaging the knuckles of one hand with the fingertips of the other, elegant in his dark suit. I pictured the truck driving Bellen into Bethlehem, the man at the wheel not a terrorist or a fanatic but a strange kind of accomplice. Voss had gone silent and now he watched his feet on the uneven ground, then looked up as if to survey the landscape with fresh eyes. "I never knew this place was actually here," he said, amused. We were almost all the way down the hill-

Creek bed, Valley of Elah

side. Between the rocks jutted thorny weeds with flowers like yellow explosions. The creek bed was choked with dead grass and thistle almost chest high. There was a culvert made of concrete and steel. Voss kicked aside some litter, a potato chip bag, then picked up a stone. You couldn't go into that dry creek bed and not pick up a stone.

"If you want to go to Tel Aviv, I'll explain more," he said.

"I thought you were the one who cared only about the facts."

"That's not the kind of piece you're interested in."

"How do you know?"

He gestured at the empty landscape and let the stone fall. "Look where we are. Not exactly an essential stop."

10) JET LAG

Around eight o'clock that night, we woke up in my hotel room — or rather, I woke up — Voss was already sitting in the chair by the window, reading. Still jet-lagged, feeling drugged by it, I could have slept much longer. I had dreamed of violent attacks on villages in the desert, men on camels setting tents on fire, hacking at people with machetes. The shades were drawn, and in the faint ring of yellow light from a single lamp, Voss looked like some otherworldly functionary scanning the newspaper in his suit and large black shoes. We'd had a drink in the bar — a club soda for Voss, who doesn't drink liquor — and I said that I needed a shower, and he'd simply nodded, holding his ground. I'd seen this coming since that moment I'd slipped on the path at Tel Azeka and he'd caught my arm. He reached his hand out now to pay for the drinks and I stopped him, putting my hand on top of his. His hair had been tousled outside and it gave him a preoccupied, middle-aged look, especially with his suit, which was still remarkably clean. In the elevator upstairs we didn't look at each other, much less touch, nor did we talk. It was as we stepped into the room that he reached for me. I was wet before he reached for me. He shut the door and we kissed, Voss pulling my face to his. Either you'll trust me for telling you even this, or you'll distrust me for telling you even this. It had something to do with the way he carried himself, his wariness. He seemed to be always signaling that he was a corrupt person, that he had degraded himself. He knew this was attractive but that didn't mean it was an act. There are men who think about their own body in addition to yours. Voss wasn't one of them. He came at me thinking about only one thing.

"You're still here," I said now. "I thought you would have left."

He didn't answer.

"I'll put this moment in the piece too," I said.

"Why?"

"Because it happened. Because it sheds light on everything else."

The room was a tranquilizing blend of contemporary patterns and Levantine colors — black and red and gold. I had a Hebrew name, Voss said — why had I never been to Israel? It was a long story, I answered. He asked if I had been to Yad Vashem, the Holocaust memorial, and I told him no, I had no real interest in it. He said I should see it.

We made plans to go see it together after we finished the story.

11) BATHSHEBA

Ivan Schwebel paints the episode many different ways, but my favorite paintings are not of Bathsheba but of her wronged husband, Uriah. Almost the first thing David does as king in his new capital, Jerusalem, is to betray one of the very men who had helped him in his rise: he sees the naked Bathsheba and he sends his men for her. Jerusalem and all it might mean — shelter, peace, a unified state, his own glory or God's — is something he seems compelled to throw away. Uriah "lay at the entrance to the king's house with all the servants of his master," loyally guarding the palace. Inside, David is sleeping with Bathsheba. She becomes pregnant. When that happens, David has to try very hard to get Uriah to sleep with her too, to hide his own paternity, but Uriah refuses to leave his post. "The Ark and Israel and Judah are sitting in huts," he says, "and my master Joab and my master's servants are encamped in the open field, and shall I then come to my house to eat and drink and to lie with my wife? By your life, by your very life, I will not do this thing."

David gets him drunk. In one of Schwebel's renderings, Uriah is a smiling young IDF private dressed in green fatigues and cap, still unshaven from the battlefront. He's seated at a table before a glass of wine, and the David who coaxes him toward drunkenness, hand on Uriah's shoulder, is a gray-haired man in the open-necked sport shirt and white slacks of a corrupt city councilman or an aging mobster. Even drunk, Uriah refuses to leave his post. The solution David comes up with is to write a letter to his commanding general, Joab: "Put Uriah in the face of the fiercest battling and draw back, so that he will be struck down and die." Uriah is killed by the Philistines. This is to say that he dies from multiple contusions, bludgeoned or stabbed, perhaps trampled on the ground by horses. The IDF has never released photographs of David Bellen's mutilated corpse. They identified it by the cards in his wallet. Bald and stocky, Bellen lamented, caustically, the frequently unbridgeable distance between himself and the beautiful young women he would see on the beach in Tel Aviv. He wrote that they liked "gold rope, barbed wire tattoo / the high sheen of / the Kid with his shirt off." In his poems, Bellen never condemns David, even for ordering the murder of Uriah. If anything, Bellen seems to admire David for his ruthless vitality. It's not hard to see how this very admiration, expressed without piety or reverence, might have gotten Bellen killed.

12) THE SON

I went with Voss to visit Bellen's son, Eliav, in his shop in the mountain town of Tsfat, near the Golan Heights and the border with Lebanon. Tsfat, an odd mix of Hasidim and New Age hippies, has been a center of Jewish mysticism since the fifteenth century, a place where revered kabbalists founded small synagogues that are still there today. Eliav's shop, like many in the town, deals in Jewish-themed art in a kitsch style loosely derived from Chagall. On either side of the entrance hung multicolored amulets called *hamsas* in the shape of disembodied hands meant to ward off the evil eye. As Bellen's only child, Eliav had come into possession of his father's effects after he died. On our drive up from Jerusalem, Voss had told me that Eliav's sale of much of this inheritance, after years of personal problems, including long struggles with drug addiction, had financed the shop in Tsfat.

Eliav Bellen is tall and thin, and because his hair is shaved down to stubble he looks somewhat spectral, even in the brightly colored Pop Art T-shirt he wore that day. I thanked him for meeting with us and he neither smiled nor spoke but gruffly nodded at me as if my gratitude was understood. Perhaps he thought it was also understood that I would share his belief that his father's murder was the work of militant right-wing Jews. He showed me some of the letters and e-mails his father had received in the nine months between the publication of *Kid Bethlehem* and his murder, most of the correspondence in Hebrew but a fair amount of it in English. The ignorance, stated in blunt, ungrammatical fragments, conjured in me the same impression of madness as certain photographs of ultra-Orthodox Jews in skullcaps and side curls shouting at Palestinians whose fields they have just burned to the ground.

I looked at Voss, whose face was blank. Eliav began a roll call of Jewish terrorists, starting with Yigal Amir, the fanatic who had murdered the prime minister, Yitzhak Rabin. He mentioned Baruch Goldstein, the right-wing zealot who had killed twenty-nine praying Muslims in a mosque in the Cave of the Patriarchs. He mentioned a left-leaning political scientist and professor named Zeev Stern-hell who had been injured the year before by a pipe bomb delivered to his home. (In the months since my return from Israel, an American-born Jewish terrorist named Yaa-kov Teitel was arrested for this incident, as well as a string of attacks against "Arab, gay, and leftist targets.")

"The last time I spoke to my father was about three days before the murder," Eliav said. "It was sometime in the afternoon. He was cooking at home, then going to a bar he liked, probably on Lilienblum Street."

He said that two or three times a month his father would take a woman to a restaurant or a bar in his neigh-borhood or farther north, on Rothschild Boulevard or Lil-ienblum Street, meeting these women either at the university where he taught or on a website on which Bel-len made no effort to conceal anything about himself. Eliav said he thought the women might even have had something do with inciting the murder. He speculated that there was usually an element of sexual frustration in terrorism — "didn't I think so?" Terrorism was sexual frus-tration blown up to a messianic scale. It was a puritanical impulse. To a person like this, Eliav said, maybe nothing could be uglier than a sixty-five-year-old man having a drink in a bar with an attractive young woman.

Voss was staring down at his knee toward the end of this. He seemed impatient to say something, but was restraining himself.

"He had habits, he was known in places, he wasn't secre-tive," I said. "Easy for someone to know where he'd be."

Eliav raised his eyebrow and sighed. "Tel Aviv is sleazy,

it's modern, it's not picturesque like Jerusalem," he said. "But it's secular. You should spend more time in Tel Aviv. If there's a future for Israel, it's Tel Aviv, not Jerusalem."

"And do you think your father thought that?"

"No, my father would say that's wistful. My father thought everything was doomed."

"And you? Why did you leave Tel Aviv? Why did you come to Tsfat?"

He looked at the paintings on the walls and extended his hands. "I'm just a peddler," he said. "I'm not peddler enough for Tel Aviv."

Whether or not Eliav had fully given up drugs, I couldn't know. Like Tsfat itself, I found him oppressive. When I asked him about the paintings, he went on to tell me that he believed in God — though the God he believed in was a figure of fear. In God's eyes, he said, we were always a disappointment. We were disappointing because He had made us in His own image. He said that when intelligent people scoffed at the idea of God they were really only scoffing at a harmless cliché. Voss had gone outside for a cigarette. I could see his arm and the sole of his shoe, which he rested, his knee bent, on the edge of the open doorframe. The last thing Eliav told me was about an appearance his father had made on the campus of the University of Michigan when Eliav was a student there. At the back of the audience, there was a young man who started making strange sexual noises as soon as Bellen began his reading. The noises started out as a low hum or whine, then grew louder and louder until a few people turned around to locate their source. Suddenly, chairs were scattered at the back of the hall. A scrum of men stood above the boy, who was struggling on the floor, barking and screaming. It took eight people to subdue him, though he was only a bookish nineteen-year-old. In the midst of a psychotic break, the boy bit their hands, scratched their faces, kicked out in powerful bursts using both legs at the same time. Bellen had seen the boy at a tea beforehand, and, noticing his peculiar affect, he'd told Eliav that he had a feeling that something would go wrong once he began his reading.

"What I'm saying," Eliav went on, "is that my father identified the boy as a kind of fanatic just by looking at him. He was a magnet for that kind of thing."

"Even in America," I said.

"My father was attuned to the violence inside people."

13) THE CYCLE

The child David conceives with Bathsheba dies. As he's mourning the loss, one of his sons, Amnon, seduces and rapes one of David's daughters, Tamar. "And Amnon hated her with a very great hatred, for greater was the hatred with which he hated her than the love with which he loved her." Amnon sends Tamar away and she "put ashes on her head, and the ornamented tunic that she had on she tore, and she put her hand on her head and walked away scream-ing." David does nothing about this violation. It's as if he recognizes his own sin against Uriah in his son Amnon's sin. It is left to another of his sons, Absalom, to avenge Tamar. "And there was no man so highly praised for beauty as Absalom in all Israel — from the sole of his foot to the crown of his head, there was no blemish in him."

Before long, the beautiful Absalom will be leading a popular uprising against his father, who no longer looks like the boy with the slingshot but more like the monster Goliath.

14) LILIENBLUM ST.

I saw a little of Tel Aviv over the next few days. I was alone, because Voss had to work in Jerusalem. He had barely been able to contain his loathing for Eliav Bellen, and when I asked him why, he told me that practically everything Eliav had said during the interview was a lie. He said that he'd interviewed a few of David Bellen's friends — Bellen did not have many, Voss said — and by all accounts the poet was something of a recluse. It had been years since he'd made a habit of going for a drink on Rothschild Boulevard or Lilienblum Street. He was more likely to stay in his apartment, where he hoarded newspapers, books, records, and DVDs. His decades-long work with a peace group that had brought together Jewish and Arab writers was over. The Arab writers had left the group in protest of the Gaza blockade. Eliav was a junkie, a thief, a heartbreak — they had been more or less estranged ever since his son's late twenties. If they'd patched things up in recent years, none of Bellen's friends had heard of it.

Heavy curtains blacked out the sun. We were in Caesarea after seeing Eliav, at the branch of the Dan Hotel there, a few hours' drive from Tsfat. When I came back out of the shower, Voss was watching the news in bed, the sheet pulled up to his waist. There was a fight at the Knesset — he hardly looked at me. I sat reading in the lobby that night. It could have been 1972. There were ashtrays by the elevator with clean white gravel inside, an abandoned bar in gloomy shadow, a bright foyer leading to an empty health club and pool.

In Tel Aviv, I thought about Voss more than I wanted to. He was my guide and my interpreter, and I was waiting for him. On my second day, I went down to the hotel lobby to check my e-mail and again there was nothing from him. He had not left any messages at the front desk. I did a search on "Oded Voss." I brought up images of his face and I clicked through some of his articles. I looked up "oded voss first lebanon war" and retrieved an article called "Ten Years After, IDF Veterans Remember" in which he was quoted: "We kept living. We even started to enjoy ourselves. I used to wonder, was it the same as forgiving myself? Now I wonder if it matters. I think, to whom could it matter?"

I didn't call or e-mail him. In my hotel room, I looked down at the sunbathers and watched generic VH1-style Israeli pop. Tel Aviv was New York, Miami, anywhere. It made me nostalgic for Jerusalem and its impassioned historical people who wanted to kill each other.

On that second night, I went out in the dark and walked up Frishman Street to Ben Yehuda, Dizengoff, then over to Allenby. Beyond the glass towers along the beach, the buildings seemed to erode beneath graffiti and Xeroxed ads for nightclubs. It took me a long time, but I walked all the way to Lilienblum, a street in a quiet neighborhood with a few discreet bars, some without signs, the kind of places journalists and writers tend to gather — chintz couches, dim lighting, music just abrasive enough to conjure youth. I asked some customers if they knew anything about David Bellen. I asked the bartenders. I showed them Bellen's picture — the glasses, the stark bald head — and none of them remembered seeing him anywhere but in the newspapers or on TV. On my way back home, a drunk came out of nowhere and started shouting that I was a whore.

You had to like modern Tel Aviv better than Jerusalem with its ancient strife. Either that, or you had to stop thinking about it.

15) VOSS

We met for lunch the next day. He said there were reasons he hadn't called but he didn't want to get into them now. He apologized for disappearing — it was inconsiderate, but perhaps I understood, perhaps in the past I'd been inconsiderate to someone myself. I assumed he meant he'd been with another woman. We ate at a café up the beach from the Dan Hotel, rows of tables and wicker chairs, oil lamps in glass boxes. He wore black jeans and an olive-colored leather jacket over a black T-shirt. He was watching me eat, sitting back a little from the table, smoking. He said he'd had to think a long time about whether he should show me the part of the city he was going to show me. He said that the reason he was going to show me was his belief in my respect for David Bellen.

"I respect him, but I don't like that word," I said. "It has a pious ring."

"It's actually very simple."

"Respect for the dead."

"Simpler than that."

"I don't know how you get any simpler than that."

He looked out at the beach. When the bill came, he put his fingers down over the leather folder and said something to the waiter in Hebrew.

16) GANGSTERS

Like a Legend from My Youth

How the mighty have fallen
in the midst of battle!
Call the old steakhouse on
Etzel Street
and tell them
Aslan the King is dead

Tell the widow
and the Alperon gang
the Three Clans
and the Mayor of Tel Aviv
Tell the orphan and the starlet that
Aslan the King is dead

In what distant deeps or skies
burnt the fire of thine eyes?
Ze'ev Rosenstein,
the Wolf with Seven Lives,
you hit the King
who nine bullets before had survived

Aslan the King is dead

17) ORIGINS

We drove to Bellen's childhood neighborhood, a working-class district called Hatikvah on the other side of Tel Aviv's main highway where the streets get narrower and closer together. Low rectangular buildings of gray concrete led into empty lanes. Shop fronts, faded awnings, dumpsters, trees like thin misplaced weeds. In Hatikvah, Voss told me, Bellen's father had sold produce in the market stalls, a Galician refugee in a district largely populated by dark-skinned Jews from Arab countries, Mizrahim. More to the point, Voss explained, Hatikvah was a center of organized crime, as it still is. I was relieved to learn that this was what Voss had been afraid to show me, why he had disappeared. Israel has already had its share of bad press. He was trusting me not to senselessly add to the noise.

We parked off Etzel Street, the setting of Bellen's poem about the famous gangster Yehezkel Aslan, the one "who nine bullets before had survived." Two old men sat outside at a plastic table with coffee and cigarettes as if they'd been sitting there all morning and would sit there tomorrow and every day thereafter. One was toothless and wore a stocking cap. The other was robust, potbellied, his shirt unbuttoned to reveal a white undershirt beneath. They looked like figures in an Ivan Schwebel painting, except they had dark skin — I thought they were Arabs but Voss made it clear to me that they were Jews. He did this by translating some graffiti on a phone booth nearby. *There will be peace when the last Arab is dead.*

We met a man whose name I can't give. What I can say is that he was in his midsixties, a white-haired man with thick eyebrows and dark skin, an Iraqi Jew, like the famous Aslan. It struck me that, like Bellen's son, Eliav, this man had an affection for the hand-shaped amulets called *hamsas*. They were all over the walls of his office, along with portraits of a Sephardic holy man with a narrow wizened face, a gray beard, a scarf covering his head like a shawl — a man whose beatific strangeness reminded me of a Sufi mystic or a fundamentalist mullah. Voss introduced me as the American journalist writing about David Bellen. The man nodded his understanding. We sat down and a boy in a green Adidas tracksuit served us pastries and black coffee. He stood in the corner of the room and watched me mostly, his hands balled in front of his waist, a gold rope chain around his neck. Moroccan-sounding music played from a radio. The room was hot and flies alighted on the sticky plastic tablecloth. The coffee came in tiny gilt-edged cups rich with Arabic-looking ornament. I understood that whatever I thought of as a "Jew" was now so broad a concept as to be meaningless.

"He and Bellen were boyhood friends," Voss explained to me. "Friends until they were about nine or ten, then there was a drifting apart."

The man told an odd story about a birthday party Bellen's parents had given for their son when the man and Bellen were growing up. It wouldn't have been much, the man said — maybe a small cake, maybe just some watermelon. It wouldn't have been much, but for the man's parents it was "like they were inviting me to a brothel." I couldn't quite understand what this meant — it had something to do with his parents' indigence, their pride in the face of what they perceived as the Bellens' softness.

The man left school to sell laundry soap in the market. He made his money now as a loan shark.

"When was the last time you saw Bellen?" I asked.

Voss translated and the man shook his head briefly and didn't answer. I asked him if he had read Bellen's poetry and instead of answering the man spat on the floor. It was not easy as a woman or an American to press him further and I began to resent Voss a little, for though he was helping me he was also inevitably policing the conversation.

"I felt very bad about what happened to him," the man said. "He was like a child — even as a sixty-five-year-old man he was like a child. To go as far away from this place as he did and then to write that book. Writing nonsense about this world he knew nothing about. Only a child would do something like that."

18) THE FIRST LEBANON WAR

After this meeting, I asked Voss a question I shouldn't have asked, a question that emerged spontaneously in a larger conversation about the history of violence that seemed to surround us everywhere. We were at a restaurant on Etzel Street, the famous steakhouse that had been owned by Yehezkel Aslan, the "King" in Bellen's poems. On the walls were signed photographs of Israeli actors and politicians, athletes, journalists. Yehezkel Aslan had run an international gambling empire worth millions of dollars, financed by loan sharking and heroin. In 1993, he was murdered outside the Pisces restaurant after surviving nine bullets to the face some years earlier. A thousand people came to his funeral. He was a folk hero, a supporter of youth athletic teams and the builder of a drug rehab center for the very addicts he had helped supply. A figure out of mythology, like King David or Tony Montana, only real.

I asked the question I shouldn't have asked, and Voss said yes, he had killed someone, he had been in a war. When I asked him to tell me the circumstances, he shook his head.

"I don't talk about that," he said. "Why would you want to talk about it?"

"Eliav Bellen said that his father thought everything was doomed. I wonder what you think about that."

"Eliav was talking about himself. Not his father."

"I'm asking about you."

"David Bellen didn't write poems because he thought everything was doomed."

"And what about you?"

"I live here. I don't think everything is doomed either."

We asked our waiter if he had ever heard of David Bellen. The waiter told us yes, David Bellen had eaten here every few weeks right up to his death.

"He liked to have lunch here and then he would walk around the neighborhood, the market," he said. "Most people didn't know who he was. He was very quiet, almost invisible. He didn't want us to put his picture on the wall."

19) A SUICIDE

Voss had brought a small suitcase this time with a few changes of clothes. We went swimming in the Mediterranean and then sat beneath an orange umbrella on rented chairs and I drank a Gold Star beer and Voss drank a club soda with a certain amount of rue. He told me about an Arab friend he'd had during his twenties when he'd lived here in Tel Aviv. It was after the war, and he and the friend had shared a bright cynicism toward anything more serious than what we saw before us now — people swimming, people laughing and smoking and having picnics on the sand. Lots of drinking, lots of drugs, lots of girls. The friend owned horses now, which he kept stabled in the Galilee. He drove a cab and had a wife and three kids, and he and his brother bred Arabian stallions for the track. He and Voss both lived in Jerusalem now, but they never saw each other. They hadn't spoken in years. It was not because of politics, but because "Ali is still married and I'm not."

I told Voss a story about an Arab cabdriver I'd had on my way from Jerusalem to Tel Aviv. On the way is a town called Abu Ghosh which is famous for its hummus. I asked the driver about why the hummus was so famous and he looked at me in silence. It turned out that he thought I was asking about Hamas, not hummus. Eventually we laughed. Voss laughed a little when I told him this story. We went back in the water and I thought everything between us was fine. He put his hands on my hips and I floated.

In my room, I had drawn the sheer curtain which let some sunlight come in — the other choice was total darkness. *I don't talk about that. Why would you want to talk about it?* The room was beige and clean and smelled like the salt water on our towels. Voss couldn't concentrate. I tried to help him. It was when I moved down his stomach that it happened. It happened so quickly that I thought something had been shot through the window.

I lay with my hand pressed to the side of my mouth, my lip and the inside of my cheek bleeding. My jaw rang. I don't think Voss knew what he'd done. He turned on his side and grasped both my wrists in his hands. "Bad luck," he said. "You can put this in the piece too." He was holding my wrists very tightly, a blank anger in his eyes, which seemed unseeing. I don't know why, but I thought of the Church of the Nativity in Bethlehem. We had driven there, I and the tourists and the driver with the cell phone that played "Careless Whisper." It was a dim place hung with censers and shabby brass lamps. I waited in line to see the manger, but the crowd was so thick that I hardly bothered to crouch down and peer into what was nothing more than a little shelf in the stone.

He brought his hand to my face and wiped my lip and I didn't know if he was going to hit me again or not. I could see that he didn't know either.

20) KILLING TIME

I went for a long walk up Rothschild Boulevard the next morning, then I took a taxi back to Jerusalem. I had two days left before my flight home. The driver wondered why I had never been to Israel before. He asked if I'd been to Yad Vashem, the Holocaust memorial, and when I told him no he insisted that I should see it. Perhaps the reason I have never wanted to face too directly the idea of myself as a Jew is that all roads seem to lead to the Holocaust memorial, as if it is the Holocaust that makes one a Jew. I knew I would not be seeing Voss here again. Perhaps that's why I ended up going to Yad Vashem that day.

Adolf Eichmann remembers: *The truck was making for an open ditch, the doors were opened, and the corpses were thrown out, as though they were still alive, so smooth were their limbs. They were hurled into the ditch, and I can still see a civilian extracting the teeth with tooth pliers.*

The tooth pliers bring it into focus. At Yad Vashem, what brought it into focus was a chart displaying locks of human hair. They illustrated the decadence in color gradations from Aryan gold to Semitic brown. I watched a video of Hitler giving a speech to a hall full of adulators. I watched a video of limp corpses being bulldozed into a trench. Black walls enclosed everything at harsh diagonals. I thought, this place has to exist but I don't know what good it can possibly do. I went into a circular room with hundreds of black phone books full of names of the dead. A girl tourist walked around in a wet-eyed angry daze. I don't cry very much. I cried when I saw her.

21) ECSTASY

There is a strange scene in the Bible when Saul, David's predecessor as king, is pursuing David through the wilderness, trying to kill him. Saul learns that David is in a village called Naioth with the prophet Samuel. "And Saul sent messengers to take David, and they saw a band of prophets in ecstasy with Samuel standing poised over them, and the spirit of God came upon Saul's messengers and they, too, went into ecstasy." Saul dispatches more messengers, and they go into ecstasy. A third band is sent and they also go into ecstasy. It is unclear what it means to be "in ecstasy." Finally Saul himself goes to Naioth and he "walked along speaking in ecstasy...and he, too, stripped off his clothes, and he, too, went into ecstasy before Samuel and lay naked all that day and all that night."

In one of Ivan Schwebel's paintings, David is dancing on a railway platform where cars are being loaded for transport to Auschwitz. He is naked, dancing in ecstasy. I wish I could talk to Voss about this. I would have liked to tell him that I think one of the points of Bellen's book is that David was Yehezkel Aslan and he was Tony Montana, but he was also "one who wrestles with God." To be that alive is to consume everything, even Auschwitz, and it is also to send for Bathsheba, simply because you can. Three thousand years ago, David, according to the tradition, was the poet who wrote the Psalms. Even if you can't believe that someone named David literally wrote the Psalms, the fact is that someone wrote them. I wonder if anyone in the world now is writing words of such resonance.

22) NOT THAT KIND OF PIECE

...by returning to that neighborhood, Bellen was offering himself up. He thought he could escape and be a prize-winning poet and this would somehow change things, but of course it didn't. It didn't change anything, so he came back in defeat. Drawn back to the place that never cared if he escaped or not. He arranges a deal—his letters and papers, worth more when he's dead, sold through someone

who could get their full worth, someone from his old neighborhood. Proceeds will go to the useless son. The son has
no idea about any of this. Any number of scenarios after
that. Maybe Bellen's broker/collaborator is so disgusted by
the idea of Bellen contemplating all this that he kills Bellen
himself, just because he can. Maybe that was somehow implied in their conversation all along. Maybe Bellen killed
himself. Maybe they drove him to Beit Sahour and let him
blow his own brains out behind a construction site. Maybe
they let him do it in Tel Aviv. The people I'm talking about
can arrange these things anywhere. They hate the Arabs
but they also work with the Arabs. Was it Bellen's inspiration or theirs to dump the body in Beit Sahour?

I can't say for certain who sent me this e-mail, which
came from a strange address, though of course I have a
guess. I haven't heard again from Voss in the eight months
since my return to New York.

23) THE CITY OF DAVID

Just before I left for Israel last May, the *New York Times*
ran a piece about the City of David, a joint effort between
the Israeli government and a private group called Ir David
to turn this section of Jerusalem into a tourist zone based
on the premise that it is the "ancient ridge where King
David is said to have conquered an existing stronghold
and laid the foundations of Jewish Jerusalem 3,000 years
ago." The article reported that "garbage dumps and
wastelands are being cleared and turned into lush gardens and parks, now already accessible to visitors who

can walk along new footpaths and take in the majestic views." The piece also discussed the removal of Palestinians who live in the area, an impoverished district called Silwan, in order to create, in the words of a peace activist, "an ideological tourist park that will determine Jewish dominance in the area." A picture emerged in the article of a project combining gentrification, tourism, and archaeology as a means of making it "harder than ever to divide Jerusalem as part of a two-state solution."

The site was partly open during my trip. There was a courtyard full of Israelis singing loud songs in Hebrew, a beautiful girl soldier with a machine gun. On the road that led to the ticket booth, a wall had been erected to screen out the ongoing construction in Silwan. Painted on the wall was a cheerful mural showing a father and son riding the two-wheeled motorized scooters called Segways, a view of the Old City behind them.

You buy your ticket and walk down steep stairs through the archaeological excavation — cisterns and baths made of quarried stone. At the bottom is the entrance to Hezekiah's Tunnel, an underground passage that leads to the biblical Pool of Siloam, the source of ancient Jerusalem's water ever since the days of the Jebusites. Your admission fee buys you a tiny LED flashlight the size of a quarter. For whatever reason, I was the only one there that morning. The water at the mouth of the tunnel rushed so quickly over the slick stones that it seemed dangerous, even impassable, and I hesitated for a while before wading in up to my knees and proceeding slowly forward into the entrance. The tunnel is 500 meters long but it feels much longer once you're inside it. It makes a sharp left turn and then it's absolutely pitch dark inside. In 700 BC, King Hezekiah's engineers began digging at either side of the cavern and managed somehow to meet in the middle — with the aid of the flashlight you can still see the marks of their tools. Someone yodeled in the distance far behind me. I kept walking, the walls hardly much wider than the width of my body and the ceiling so low I had to crouch. I felt that if my flashlight went out or I dropped it, I would be lost there for a long time. The water rushed at my ankles and the way ahead got narrower and more jagged. In a tunnel that narrow, you can't turn around because you can't pass anyone coming the other way. You have to walk to the end. The yodeling was muffled and eerie. The darkness was so total that it made no difference if you closed your eyes or opened them. I turned off my flashlight for a moment and stood there taking it in.

9

Immigrants, Part 3

1972/2010

He didn't know where he would live now, maybe Paraguay — some visas had been arranged there, though he knew almost nothing about the country and was afraid to think about it. It was November 5, 1972, two months after he'd lost his case before the Israeli supreme court, just five days before the expulsion order was to go into effect, and he sent some bags ahead with a friend, then traveled alone that night from Tel Aviv to Zurich, where the friend met him with boarding passes and transit visas to Asunción, Lansky's documents under the name "Mr. Meyer." Gray suit, dress shirt from Brooks Brothers, madras tie — he was already sticky under his clothes by the time the plane had left Lod. They made it across the Atlantic that night to Rio de Janeiro, then caught a connection to Buenos Aires a few hours later the same morning. Israel, Switzerland, Brazil, Argentina. Soiled from the stuffy cabin air, waiting for the flight to Paraguay, he decided to get a shave in the airport barbershop. It was just hours later, when they landed in Asunción, that he realized the plan had failed. Two Paraguayans, then an American agent of some kind, came into the cabin and said in English that he was not permitted to disembark. It turned out that the flight to Asunción had further stops in La Paz, Lima, Panama City, and finally Miami. It turned out that all the FBI had to do, once he'd boarded in Buenos Aires, was to keep him on the plane all the way to its terminus. America. Thirty-six hours in transit, stops in seven countries. They met him at Miami International and drove him to the FBI office downtown, where his lawyer went out to get him a piece of bread and some milk for his ulcers.

———

In her living room on Long Island, Gila read the letter another time, then folded it into thirds and put it into the envelope. She turned down the stereo and stood there with her eyes closed, waiting. She was going to mail it care of Hannah Groff's editor but you didn't have to do that anymore. It was 2010 and Hannah of course had her own website. Her address was right there on the website. She put the stamp on the letter and left it on the sideboard and went into the kitchen for a glass of water and took the morning's dose of aprepitant, which helped with the nausea during her chemotherapy treatments. She ran some cool water over her face in the kitchen sink, pressing her fingertips to her eyes. It had been twenty-eight years since she'd seen Hannah. Maybe they could talk now. They could talk about some of the things Hannah didn't know — they could talk about Meyer.

Forty minutes sitting with her hands over her face, trying not to vomit. She took another shower and the lavender scent of the soap was mild enough to be soothing. The silk pajamas hurt her skin, so she put on some cotton ones. She looked at the letter on the sideboard, then she went back again to Hannah's story about David Bellen.

10

Reunion

NEW YORK, 2010

1.

I received Gila Konig's first letter in the spring of 2010, about six months after my piece on David Bellen had first been published. Apart from the Bellen story, I hadn't written any of the book you're reading now — I didn't know yet that the Bellen piece would become part of the larger story I would eventually, after some resistance, find myself telling. As I said before, when Gila told me about her past in Tel Aviv in 2010, I knew almost nothing about Meyer Lansky and wasn't very interested in him.

I saw her only one time after I was twelve, at a restaurant on 79th Street, just a few blocks from where my father had run his antiques business back in 1982, the last time we'd seen each other. It was a bright sunny afternoon and Gila wore a cream-colored hat made of soft straw to protect her skin from the sun. That May, at the age of seventy-one, she had undergone what would turn out to be her final round of radiation and chemotherapy treatments. Her hair beneath the hat had started to grow back in, gray and straight and close to the scalp. I had forgotten the delicateness of her cheekbones, her lips. We sat upstairs on the restaurant's covered porch, fans hung from the ceiling, waiters moving by in white jackets, as in some old film whose setting was Capri. I smiled at Gila the way I sometimes cry at a movie that isn't really sad. She had written me a few times now. I imagined her motives for seeking me out were bound up in her illness. Because I write for a living, people I don't know or hardly know have frequently approached me on the slimmest of pretexts to set down their life stories. It just happens, more than I would have ever expected. Particularly in the face of illness or old age, they come to me with secrets that no longer seem important enough to be ashamed of. I listen to the crux of their lives and I tell them no, I'm sorry, I'm busy with other projects. What I can't explain is that it's not that their life story isn't interesting, it's that everyone's life story is interesting.

But Gila was of course someone I knew. A friend of hers, she'd told me, had seen my piece on Bellen and passed it on to her — the friend, Hugh, and his partner owned the apartment where Gila was staying that night as a guest. They had a summer house near where Gila lived now, in Sag Harbor, New York. It was a strange coincidence, I pointed out — my family, as she knew, had had a house in the next town over, Southampton. As she also knew, it was during a stay at that house that my father had first told me of their affair.

Her clothes looked expensive — pearl-gray slacks, a simple white blouse, crisply pressed. The clothes seemed to assert that she had taste and also more money than I probably expected.

"'Strange,'" she said, echoing my word. "Everyone always says 'strange.' But life is strange. My life certainly has been strange."

She took a slow drink of water. When she put the glass down, she lightly wiped her hands, one atop the other, watching them. The cancer had been "strange," she told me. It had started in her big toe — all her toenails turned a cloudy white — and two different doctors had assured her at first that it was nothing, until by the time anyone gave it any real thought it had metastasized all over her body.

I said I was sorry. She looked at me then with something like forbearance, a kind of suppressed disappointment. In that look, I could see a regret for all the perfectly real things that separated us. But I could also see that, having read my piece, she thought we were somehow kindred spirits. She had expected something less trite from me than "strange" and "I'm sorry."

"I didn't ask you here to talk about what happened with your father all that time ago," she said then. "A lot of painful things. Obviously. And I didn't ask you here to talk about my cancer. A lot of people get cancer. I wanted to show you something. That's why I asked you here. This is something I thought you'd find interesting as a writer. Something that's not just personal."

With some difficulty, she took an old photo album out of her purse. It contained a fading collection of 5x7 prints that dated back to the 1970s, their colors degrading into an acidic murk behind their plastic compartments. She showed me one series in particular — I wish I had the photographs with me now — first through the plastic, then, so I could get a better look, removing the pictures from the album. They were stark interior views of an apartment, like realtor's photos, except that these photos made no attempt to flatter the space they portrayed. The ceilings were low, the light depressingly dim. There was no furniture. The apartment was an empty shell with scuff marks on the walls where pictures might once have hung.

"It's the one I told you about in my last letter," she said. "It's on a nice street, it must be worth some money these days. As I told you, I could have been living there right now, living there all this time. That was the idea."

The apartment was a few miles from the hotel where she had worked for many years in Tel Aviv, the Dan. That was where she'd met Meyer Lansky, she said, bringing him coffee in the downstairs lobby.

She introduced me to a Hebrew word then, *yored*. Its root means "to descend." It's what Israelis are called when they leave and go to another country. They have "descended." They have gone down to the corrupt world outside, so to speak, abandoned the holy land that is their rightful home.

"Strange," she said again. "I don't know how my friend Hugh found your story, but these things happen. He knew about my life in Tel Aviv, and so he passed it on. And then everyone says 'strange.' 'How strange.'"

She showed me another photograph. This one was of her mother, a thin woman in a bright orange head scarf, her pale skin lusterless, like clear wax. Of course I already knew something about Gila's mother, in particular about what Gila's mother had done to keep them both alive during their time in Bergen-Belsen.

"She's sixty-four in that picture," Gila said. "She had cancer too. I took care of her for eight years — she fought for a long time. When she died, in 1979, I had just turned forty. I didn't want her to die, but obviously her living meant I had to keep taking care of her. I was a cocktail waitress — the Dan Hotel is still there on the beach in Tel Aviv, you can go see it sometime. What I'm saying is that there was no way someone like me was going to make a fresh start after eight years of that. There was no way for someone like me to get ahead."

She met my eye with a defiant candor. She was telling me this story not as a woman who'd known me as a twelve-year-old girl, but as a woman who knew me now. She was tough — I'd forgotten that. I found myself feeling a complicated warmth toward her. There was of course another part of me that felt otherwise, that deeply mistrusted her. Her affair with my father, in conjunction with my mother's death, had caused all kinds of problems for me. Sometimes it seems that the confusion of that time has never really faded and that I go through life dazed — skeptical but also credulous, both doubter and believer at the same time — with the hazy result that I am almost never correct in my assessment of other people and their motives. The memory of my father telling me about their affair is a blur. The girl on the other side of the blur, the girl who was I, is not even someone I particularly like. Out of that blur comes whoever I am now. And so the blur is shaming, because it represents a force outside my control that is in a sense definitive.

The opposite of *yored*, she told me then, is *oleh* — the plural is *olim*. *Olim* are those who have "ascended" — those who have gone to Israel and settled there. "The American," as she referred to Lansky now, had wanted to become *oleh*, she said, but he was refused. This was the story she was telling me. The apartment in Tel Aviv was his parting gift, an odd gift that had made her feel somehow diminished. It seemed to imply that she needed his help, that she was incapable of taking care of herself. She still didn't know how the arrangement worked. The rent was always paid, the power stayed on, the water, the gas. No one would tell her who was keeping up these payments.

"The management company said it had been taken care of," she told me. "What else did I want to know, it was mine. Well, they knew that I knew who was ultimately taking care of it. I did know. I'd had a relationship with him. In a sense, I still had a relationship with him. This is what I meant when I talked about *yored* before. The sense of going down, of descending, of being corrupt. Both of us were *yordim*, even though I still lived in Israel, even though I was a citizen there. We would both always be *yordim*, never *olim*. That was one of the things we had in common. This is what I thought you might find interesting."

She was still striking, even in her illness. I was resisting the temptation to order a glass of wine and the effort was making my mouth a little dry. Gila seemed to sense this, watching me.

"I'm glad you came," she said. "I was worried you wouldn't, that you'd change your mind."

"It's been twenty-eight years," I said. "A long time."

"In a sense it's been a long time. But in another sense, it's like it just happened. All those things in the past. We haven't seen each other in all these years. In that sense, it's like it was yesterday."

She'd wanted to be a designer, she went on. In the seventies, in Tel Aviv, she had shown some sketches she'd made of women's clothes to a man who manufactured swimwear, but he'd been dismissive. Even after her mother's death, she'd had no real hope of getting anywhere. And yet, she told me, there was that empty apartment sitting on a quiet street in Tel Aviv which she could either live in rent-free after her mother's death or find some other way to exploit.

"I went to South Tel Aviv," she told me. "Those places you wrote about where Bellen came from — Hatikva, Etzel Street. I knew enough to know that that's where I should go. There was a cook I worked with at the hotel and he brought me — we took the bus that first time, it was a weekday, before our shift. Even back then, it was like you describe. Coffee for the men. For me, nothing. Coffee in those little gold-rimmed cups. I had to go back three or four times — it was just luck finally that got me anywhere. Luck. They wouldn't have told me a word if I hadn't recognized one of them. He'd been the driver of the man I told you about, the American. Because I knew his driver, I could speak to them. I could tell them that I didn't want the apartment. What I wanted was the next year's rent and then the apartment was theirs — whoever's. I had no idea how much the rent was. I just thought one year sounded like a nice round figure."

She assumed they would say no, or worse, that they'd ask for something back, involve her somehow, but then, after two weeks of silence, the driver appeared one evening at the Dan Hotel. He arranged to meet her the next day at the apartment she'd shared with her mother all those years.

"It was not a full year's rent," she told me. "It was more like a few months. But it was enough for an air ticket, with a little left over. It was enough to get me here."

The waiter cleared our unfinished salads. I told Gila I had to go to the bathroom, but what I really needed was to go inside and sit at the bar and write it down without her watching me. If I don't write it down, it begins to change. I knew it was changing a little even as I was writing it down. Etzel Street. Hatikva. The names of places she'd seen in my piece. I still didn't know how much I believed her story. It occurred to me that the whole time I was in Israel, I had never once thought of my old babysitter, Gila Konig.

Gila Konig, born Tsilya Konig, somewhere in Hungary, 1939. Survivor of Bergen-Belsen, survivor of a DP camp outside Munich called Foehrenwald, refugee in the new state of Israel, 1950–1980. In 1980, Gila Konig had come to New York with a few hundred dollars and no connections, thinking she might find work as a designer, or if not as a designer, doing something in the fashion industry. Eventually, with my father's help, she managed to enter into the dress business, selling wholesale to department stores — Macy's, Dillard's, Neiman Marcus — from her own small showroom on Seventh Avenue. And for a brief span early on in this trajectory — for a little more than a year — she had scraped by as a Hebrew school teacher at a temple on the Upper East Side, the congregation my family happened to belong to in the year my mother began dying of cancer.

I noticed that throughout our conversation she had almost never referred to Lansky by name. It was "the man I told you about," or "the man I knew, the American." It occurred to me that you could read this two ways. It was either an indication that she was lying and was nervous that her story sounded untrue, or that she was telling the truth and was nervous that her story sounded untrue.

When I returned to the table, she was talking on her cell phone. After she finished, there was a silence as we readjusted to the people we were now, as opposed to the people we'd been all those years ago. She looked away, at the long line of tables to our side, most of them empty. They each had a tiny white vase with a white orchid and a sprig of fern, which in the shade of the porch stood in subtle but dramatic contrast to the white tablecloths.

"I'm lucky I know Hugh," she said. "I don't have many people in my life. He's waiting for me. He's at the apartment. I'll finish telling you the story and then we should go."

She took another sip of water, as if in preparation, and then she told me what I would have guessed a long time ago if I had wanted to think about it. She told me that her affair with my father had started before my mother's death, not after it. She admitted that from the moment she'd met my father she could see what he would ultimately want. She could see the opening, I suppose you could say, but of course she put it differently. He was "lost" in "grief," she said. It wasn't what my father "wanted," it was what he "needed." It was "naïve," she went on, to wish for men to be "better" than they were. I feel somehow prim writing this all down now, inserting these quotation marks. I look at my past and what infuriates me is not my father but the rigid predictability of everything I did in the hopes of getting back at him — my marriage after a promiscuous past, the affair that then broke that marriage up. All of that by my midtwenties. All so that I could for a brief time pretend to be better than my father and then repeat the kind of behavior I held against him. When you're young, your power is self-destruction. It occurred to me that my being there at that lunch was just a late echo of that self-destruction.

"You're not angry at me," Gila said.

"I told you already, it was a long time ago."

"You haven't told me what your intentions are. What your interest in all this is."

"If you're asking if I want to write about your past, then I don't have any intentions. I have other things I'm working on right now."

"I would think there would be money in a story like this, but maybe that's a little vulgar for you, getting money for something you're not that interested in, or that wasn't your idea. I guess I think about money because I wasn't born into a world like this one, the kind of world you were born into. The kind of world your father was able to give you access to."

She sat up very straight, her hands placed before her on the table, and looked at me with something like reproach. Perhaps hearing someone's confession is inherently draining. Its effect at that moment was to prevent me from pressing her to tell me anything more. I knew that's what she wanted, and to ask would have made me feel I was indulging her, granting her story more interest than I wanted it to have. As I said, I was familiar with people overestimating the specialness of their stories. People imagine movies. They imagine a best seller, not a vanity press book. It's the way the world is, everywhere, not only in America. You can go through Bergen-Belsen, Foehrenwald, and still be prey to this myth.

I knew I couldn't write in good faith about Gila's past with Lansky without writing about her past with my father — perhaps that explains my lack of interest at that lunch. I knew that to write about my father would only be to open up the old wounds, and I'd already done some of that years before in the memoir I'd written about my marriage and its collapse. I was tired of memoirs, I thought, tired of myself. But perhaps I was simply tired of struggling with my father and his opinion of my opinions. Which is to say that it was probably inevitable that I would eventually write about Gila and Lansky, Gila and my father, for I was still angry with my father, even if I didn't want to be.

The waiter came with the bill. We weren't friends, so although I offered to help Gila with the check, I didn't press it when she refused.

"I'll tell you more the next time," she said. "When we see each other again. How about that?"

She smiled. She wanted more from me even now. She wanted the waiter to take our photograph. I forced myself to move my chair around the table, closer to Gila's, my hand on her shoulder, so he could fit us both in the frame.

"Thank you for coming," she said then, flatly.

Hearing that sudden hardness in her voice, I had a moment of regret. I began to feel that I had judged her too harshly. She took one last look at the photo on her digital camera, then drew back the lens and put it in her purse. We smiled at each other — my smile transparently false — and before saying goodbye I made an equally false promise that we'd see each other again soon.

2.

I went to visit my father a few days later. He lives now on 72nd Street, about eight blocks from where we'd lived when I was growing up. When the elevator door opens on the third floor, even when you know what to expect, the light-filled spaciousness can still come as a surprise. The living room, like a vast hall, has three different groupings of sofas and chairs — it even has one of those peculiar circular couches, usually seen in hotel lobbies, with a tall bouquet at the center like the pistil in a giant lotus. Floor lamps, framed etchings, a bronze boddhisattva standing lankily in a far corner. In the room he uses as his study, he switched off the TV and I told him about my lunch with Gila. He listened inattentively, eating cold beef consommé out of a bowl.

"She lives in Sag Harbor," I said. "Like she's been trying to get back there ever since that weekend."

He wiped his hands on a large napkin, licking his teeth. "She came in to say hello about a year ago," he said. "Right before I closed up the shop. She had cancer, she told me. They didn't know yet how serious it was. Maybe she just didn't want to tell me."

"You never told me you saw her."

"Once or twice over the years she came in to say hello."

He was even less interested in my meeting with Gila than I'd expected him to be. I understood then that he seldom if ever thinks about her, just as, in the wake of all the trouble I brought him when I was younger, he seldom thinks of me. I made it hard for him — I frustrated and ultimately baffled him. He had only wished me well all those years. I was so accusative for so long that in his eyes that's who I am now, no matter how often we see each other.

He had other problems to think about in any case. A few months before this, his name had appeared in a newspaper story along with the name of a longtime partner of his — an antiques dealer in London — who had been accused of fraud. The dealer in London had sold a consignment of English furniture to a dealer in Switzerland. My father had negotiated with this Swiss dealer to sell some of the English furniture to clients in New York. The consignment of furniture, falsely valued at over three million dollars, turned out to contain several forgeries. My father has claimed repeatedly that he had no idea about this. He "flatly denies" knowing anything about it, as the newspaper put it.

He showed me an elegant piece of furniture that afternoon — it was the massive desk in his study. It had belonged to his best friend, Harry Klein, he told me, the friend whose boat we used to go on when I was young. After Klein's death, his wife, Deborah, had found herself in financial trouble, their assets worth far less than she'd believed. The desk, my father pointed out, had ebony marquetry and fleur-de-lis spandrels flanked by pilasters carved like acanthus leaves. It was called a partners desk, he told me. There were kneeholes on all four sides of its mahogany bulk so that four bankers could sit together in the sepia light and go over accounts. He didn't know where the Kleins had found it. He asked me how much I thought it was worth, and I told him I had no idea. He said that Deborah Klein had lived with the desk for almost twenty years. It had made her feel a certain way about herself, about her life with Harry. They'd had a set of Hepplewhite chairs, a French commode from the eighteenth century, this partners desk from a famous workshop in England, Marsh & Tatham. After Harry's death, the finances unraveled. Deborah had had to sell the house in Southampton, the house I'd visited as a girl. When she asked my father for his help with the antiques, he'd had to tell her, after she'd already lost so much, that the desk too wasn't worth anything like what she'd thought. There were faded spots in the wood in places light would never have hit it. It was a fake — it had been cobbled together from scraps of other old pieces of furniture. My father gave her seventy-five thousand dollars for it, more than it was worth. She hadn't spoken to him since. She'd thought the desk was worth four times that. In Deborah Klein's mind, the desk was worth more than their friendship.

"You don't talk about yourself very much," I said.

"No. Not really."

"You think it's tasteless?"

"Something like that."

"Maybe that's why I'm curious. Because of the tastelessness."

"I don't think about the past very much. I try not to."

"Why?"

"My parents never talked about the past. My grandparents didn't. The past was what you were trying to get away from. You understand why."

"No."

"Because we came from nowhere. Because we were no one. That's why. Part of becoming someone is not having to talk about your past. I couldn't talk about it now if I wanted to. I don't know anything about it."

He had something else he wanted to share with me that afternoon, a kind of family heirloom, which he presented to me there in the study. His brother Jacob had recently passed on some recordings made by their father — my grandfather — who died before I really knew him. My grandfather had built up a chain of jewelry stores which were then fought over after his death by his two eldest sons, my uncles. They turned the chain of stores into rival boutiques that have since become famous. My father won't set foot in either of them. He feels judged by his brothers, I think, because they have made even more money than he has. I say all this, and yet after a lifetime in his company, I don't really know him. He is probably unknowable. When he says he has no information about the past, I believe him. It would have been not just personal shame his family felt, but also the greater shame of having left behind an impoverished world that eventually was exterminated. It wasn't something people talked about. Very likely, it wasn't even possible to talk about it.

He wanted to play me these recordings. He explained that his father would sometimes amuse his sons by hosting a mock radio show which he would capture on an old-fashioned gramophone that cut actual records, small shellac discs that could then be played back. My uncle had kept hundreds of these discs in storage and finally had them preserved on CDs. My father is in his mid-seventies now. He bent over the stereo with a scowl that looked angry but was really only reflexive, the face he wears when concentrating. He wore what he almost always wears in summer, a dress shirt with French cuffs, linen trousers, polished shoes. His hands shook a little. He stood there stooped over the CD player as the recordings began.

The first track was a kind of clownish singing, slightly embarrassing to hear. It was an old Broadway tune I didn't know, the lyrics adjusted into puns about my grandfather's jewelry store. My uncle — I assume it was my uncle singing — added a few bars of "The Tennessee Waltz" for some reason, letting his voice break like a yodeling cowpoke's. Then my grandfather asked some questions of another little boy in the style of a journalist:

Who is the best singer in the world?

I don't know.

Caruso?

I don't know.

My father turned and looked at me, his hand pressed against his lower back. His new wife has a house in Connecticut, an old family house, and she spends most of the weekends there. I don't think he would have been playing me these recordings if she was around. She's been around less and less since the accusations appeared in the newspaper.

"It's you," I said, meaning the voice of the little boy.

"Nineteen forty. Nineteen forty-one. Sometime before the war, I'm pretty sure."

"You sound happy."

He shrugged. I think he sensed already that I was going to write him into this book. He knew it before I did, as if my disloyalty was never in doubt. His shrug was like his resigned way of urging me not to. He had come as far a distance as Gila Konig had, I think he was telling me with that shrug. Not as a victim but as a self-invention. Not as a *yored*, but as one of the *olim* — no one was more ascended than my father in his Upper East Side town house, a world away from the Brownsville slum of his own father's youth. He had no interest in the *yordim*. I'm sure he wondered why I did.

3.

Gila sent me an e-mail after two weeks. I didn't open it at first, and when I did open it I didn't open the attachment, the photograph of us at lunch. I could see it in miniature beneath Gila's brief note. The note thanked me for having lunch with her and then extended an invitation to visit her sometime in Sag Harbor. I saw myself in the tiny photo, ghostlike, trying to hide my discomfort — I thought I would have hidden it better. The fact that Gila could have looked at that picture and still sent it to me was a poignant indicator of her aloneness. *I'm lucky I know Hugh. I don't have many people in my life.* She had waited two weeks to thank me for a lunch she had treated me to, a lunch I had never thanked her for.

The e-mail sat unanswered, shadowing me at odd times over the next few days. I don't know why I didn't want to face it. I wasn't even particularly busy. When I look back over my inbox now, I see that it took me almost three weeks to respond. I have the response here in all its vapid, agreeable insincerity:

Dear Gila,

Yes, it would be great to see you again. I have given your story and its connection to my piece about David Bellen a lot of thought. I get to the Hamptons fairly often, so I'll drop you a line the next time I'm out. Thank you for lunch, by the way.

All best,
Hannah

And now it was my turn to face the silence of an unanswered e-mail.

When she didn't respond — one week becoming two — I began to feel somehow insecure. Despite my e-mail's formal politeness, I knew it exuded an obvious lack of interest, if not outright rudeness. I hadn't trusted her, but I didn't know exactly why. Her pursuit of me had made her seem distorted, or inappropriate. But now that Gila hadn't responded to me, I began to think differently. It's the way these things go. I now thought that she had the dignity to know when she was being discounted. I considered writing her again, but I put it off. By then I was actually busy with other projects. Her silence, when I thought of it, took on a haughtiness, even a hostility. Eventually, I got a phone call not from Gila but from her friend Hugh. Gila, he told me, had passed away. It turned out she had not been avoiding my e-mail for the past three months but rather dying of cancer.

4.

She'd lived on a small side street in Sag Harbor, not far from Peconic Bay. I took the train to Bridgehampton, then a cab to the address that Hugh had given me. Gila's house had been recently painted so that its white clapboard and black shutters gleamed as if still wet. Whatever I'd expected, I had not expected the pleasant quiet of the small front yard with its weeping cherry tree, the beds of dark ivy threading upward to cover the trunks of a row of pollarded sycamores. Hugh answered the door. He was in charge of Gila's estate, including the sale of her house. He was a large man in his early fifties, his girth draped by a boxy dress shirt, pink with white stripes, the tails out over his jeans. Expensive eyewear, a very precise haircut. He invited me back into the house and in the living room he sat down in a leather armchair and lit a cigarette, asking only afterward if I minded. He spread out his hand to indicate the immaculate neatness of the place. There were no carpets on the floor, just the richly varnished wide plank boards. Plain sheer curtains hanging from black iron rods. I took a seat on a large white sofa before a coffee table made of black wood. On it rested one book, an oversized volume called *David, The King*, by Ivan Schwebel, the Israeli artist, placed there almost in vengeance, it seemed, against its qualities as an ornament. Everything was clean and so pared down that the air seemed more still than ordinary air.

"This was how she liked to live," Hugh told me.

"Spare."

"There were seven people at the funeral. She didn't like people very much. She was past all that, not interested in playing ball anymore."

He leaned back in his chair. He told me then that what he liked about Gila was "all that turmoil in her head. All that self-generated struggle. You'd give her a compliment and she'd twist it around — you were not only insulting her but patronizing her.

Thinking she was too stupid to see through your flattery. I'm a surgeon. I operate on people's spines for a living. They're spread-eagle on an inclining table for eight, ten hours. There's no room for error, obviously. It's not something I can talk about with every-one. Not even my partner. It's not something that's interesting to him. With Gila it wasn't that she was especially interested, but there was something we understood about each other. Something about work, I guess. I don't know what it was."

I asked him what she had told him about her private life.

"Not much," he said. He made a little breathing sound, some-where between a scoff and a laugh. I looked at his cigarettes and then he nodded and I took one.

"Everything was always this vague mystery," he said. "There was the designer. The swimwear designer. That was a good story — I never knew if I believed it or not, but I always liked it."

The swimwear designer, he told me, had rented Gila an apart-ment in Tel Aviv. It was their love nest, he said. Even after she broke up with him, the swimwear designer had kept paying the rent and utilities for some reason. He said that eventually Gila had sold the furniture and left the place sitting there empty. It was with that money, he told me, that she'd come from Israel to America.

I told him the very different version of the story that Gila had told me. I told him about the photographs of the empty apartment and about Gila's venture to Etzel Street, a street associated with organized crime. I told him about Meyer Lansky. I told all this to Hugh and then I asked him whether he believed any of it and he shrugged, looking not at me but at the wood floor.

"Lonely people can be difficult," he said. "When they want you around, they can be desperate to keep you there. That's why when she wanted to meet you, I encouraged her. I thought, fine, let her make the connection if she can. She needed it. She was, to put it bluntly, dying of cancer."

The sun outside found an opening between the clouds and it came streaming in through the window, lighting up a diagonal plane of swirling dust. I finished my cigarette and Hugh lit up another and we sat in silence for a while. I wasn't sure I shared his skepticism about the story Gila had told me. I wasn't sure I even believed he was giving me an accurate account of what Gila had told him. People conflate things. The "notorious" figure blurs into the "swimwear designer" when we hear a few stories and aren't paying close attention. I thought that even if that wasn't the case, it was still possible that Gila had soft-pedaled the story for Hugh. If she'd wanted to intrigue me, perhaps she'd just wanted to titillate Hugh. The more I thought about it, the more sense this made. The alternative story of the "swimwear designer," the "love nest," selling the man's furniture with an insouciant flourish, didn't sound like the Gila I had met for lunch, nor the Gila I had known all those years ago. It sounded more like someone trying to be lighter and breezier than she really was. Perhaps it had always been easier for Gila, even with a friend like Hugh, to make her story lighter, breezier than it really was.

5.

Throughout this time, I'd been traveling a lot for work — teaching at a university in Montana, another in Chicago — and when I returned to New York in the summer of 2011, after more than a year away, I felt less at home than before, a condition that has not changed. I began to feel invisible. I don't know how else to describe it. I'd begin to tell a story and lose interest halfway through. Whatever I was saying seemed unimportant or false. The people I spoke to began to seem more real than I was — by real, I mean that they seemed to occupy physical space while I hovered ghostlike, evaporating. Most of my friends had moved across the river to Brooklyn years ago. Their detailed interest in all things of the current moment induced in me a kind of hypnotic inertia. I didn't care, but I knew I needed to care. It's fine not to care until your not caring has left you so isolated that you have to either make an effort to care or you'll disappear entirely.

It was around this time that things began to deteriorate with my father. I had told him about my meeting with Hugh — I had told him I was going to write Gila's story after all. His name had appeared in the papers again. When I asked if he was worried, he told me no, he hadn't done anything wrong. When I asked him how he felt about my writing Gila's story, he was more enigmatic. He said, "You're my daughter," by which either he meant he supported me despite his qualms, or that my lack of discretion had left him speechless. Or perhaps my betrayal simply reminded him of his own.

I tell you everything, he had said that afternoon twenty-eight years ago when he'd told me about his affair with Gila. *I tell you everything, that's the rule.* I think it's an open question as to whether "telling everything" is the right thing to do. I know that ever since my father told me about Gila I have been insatiable in my need to tell everything, to expose myself and others, and I know by now that this has less to do with ethics than with the need itself.

I see now that this book is my idea of a Jewish story. It's an unflattering story, negative in many ways. I suppose it begs the question, why tell such a story? Perhaps my father has simply gotten tired of my need to tell such stories.

I continued to think about Gila. Then, about a year after my visit with Hugh, I received an e-mail from David Bellen's editor in Israel, Galit Levy.

This will interest you, she wrote. *Hope you are well.*

Part Three

World of Our Fathers

11

I Pity the Poor Immigrant
by David Bellen

Books discussed in this essay:

Havana Nocturne: How the Mob Owned Cuba and Then Lost It to the Revolution, T. J. English, William Morrow, forthcoming, 2008.

The Money and the Power: The Making of Las Vegas and Its Hold on America, 1947–2000, Sally Denton and Roger Morris, Alfred A. Knopf, 2001.

The Man Who Invented Las Vegas, W. R. Wilkerson III, Ciro's Books, 2000.

The Rise and Fall of the Jewish Gangster in America, Revised Edition, Albert Fried, Columbia University Press, 1993.

Little Man: Meyer Lansky and the Gangster Life, Robert Lacey, Little, Brown, 1991.

Meyer Lansky: Mogul of the Mob, Dennis Eisenberg, Uri Dan, and Eli Landau, Paddington Press, 1979.

The Last Testament of Lucky Luciano, Martin A. Gosch, Little, Brown, 1974.

Lansky, Hank Messick, G. P. Putnam's Sons, 1971.

He saw the world through the gangster's eye, an eye educated by long, arduous training, through the assumption of a whole system according to which mankind consists of two distinct species, wolves and lambs, predators and victims, winners and losers, deceivers and deceived—the elect and the rabble. It is the elected few, of course, who grasp the truth of this irreparable division, who possess the courage and energy to act on it. And what distinguishes gangsters, so-called, from the rest of the elect—capitalists, politicians, law-enforcers, and all the others who are successful in their putatively legitimate vocations—is that they, the gangsters, are open and aboveboard, and transparently honest with themselves, i.e., free of illusion, self-deception, and hypocrisy. So, by their own perverted logic, they, the gangsters, define themselves as the most virtuous of the elect.

Albert Fried,
*The Rise and Fall of the Jewish Gangster
in America*

PERVERTED LOGIC

In his study *The Rise and Fall of the Jewish Gangster in America,* Albert Fried reports that on October 24, 1918, the gangster Meyer Lansky, aged sixteen, "heard screams coming from an abandoned tenement house," where two boys — Benjamin Siegel and Charlie Luciano (then known as Salvatore Lucania) — were fighting over a girl. "Without a second's hesitation, Lansky leaped into the fray," Fried writes, and hit Luciano with a crowbar. The police arrived and took all three boys to the Fifth Street station house — Meyer Lansky, Bugsy Siegel, Lucky Luciano. "It marked the beginning of one of the exceptional friendships in American crime," Fried writes. His source for this, according to his own notes, is a 1971 biography-cum-pulp-novel called *Lansky* by a tabloid journalist named Hank Messick:

> Sprawled on the floor was a small black-haired boy of about twelve [Siegel]. The fly on his blue knickers was open, and his swollen penis jutted through it impressively. A girl-woman lay beside him, her skirts high enough to expose the pink bloomers beneath. Towering over both of them was Salvatore Lucania who at age twenty-one had a bad reputation. Even as Lansky watched, Lucania kicked the woman in the side.
>
> "You bitch," he shouted.
>
> And now Lansky realized the woman was laughing through her tears.
>
> "I didn't mean anything," she spluttered. "He was so cute."

The boy crawled to his feet. His face was a pale yellow, but a knife gleamed in his hand. He gathered himself into a crouch, ready to spring.

Lansky opened his toolbox and grasped a small crowbar. "Hold it," he said.

Hank Messick doesn't cite any source at all for this "re-creation," written more than fifty years after the incident allegedly happened. Albert Fried takes this already fic-tionalized scene and adds his own variants — his Lansky leaps into the fray "without a second's hesitation." There is no "toolbox" containing the "small" crowbar. A poet primarily, I simply argue that this is how myths are created, and myths, no matter how imaginary, not only distort reality but impinge upon it. My copy of *Lansky* — a mass-market paperback containing an ad for Kent ciga-rettes with a "micronite filter" — bears on its cover the slogan, *The book that tore the lid off the syndicate and forced Lansky out of Israel.* Indeed, Messick's book did help chase Lansky out of Israel, and its mythology helped to keep him for the rest of his life in a kind of personal diaspora of fantasies, rumors, wishes, fears. "A Jew has a slim chance in the world," Lansky said when the Israeli Supreme Court denied his petition for citizen-ship. It's a stunningly strange thing for a Jew in Israel to say — a Kafkaesque thing to say. It's like saying you can never live anywhere and can never learn the reason why.

THE ELECT

Wolves and lambs, predators and victims, winners and losers, deceivers and deceived. It's twenty-nine years after Lansky's expulsion — 2001, a year into the Second Intifada — and my son Eliav is wandering the streets of Tel Aviv, shifting from pile to pile, collecting bottles and cans for the deposit money so that he can buy heroin. He's a native-born Israeli, a sabra, not a Jew in some land of exile. He narrows his field of vision to the space directly in front of his feet — the gleam of schist in the pavement, the garbage sacks translucent and swelling in the sunlight — and reaches his hand into the damp opening. At night, he listens to the muffled bass of car radios and the occasional siren or helicopter, alone in a dark room with a hot plate and a water jug and a mirror and a lamp. After a while, he starts to see cans and bottles everywhere — in mud puddles and clogged sewer grates, bleached pale amid the weeds of vacant lots. After a while, it becomes a kind of challenge or a game to see what he's willing to touch with his bare hands.

LAND OF EXILE

In 2006, I go to the Lower East Side of New York, where you can visit a tenement on Orchard Street left partly in ruins, a relic of what was once the most densely populated neighborhood in the world. The entrance is dark even in the middle of the day, a small orange bulb illuminating the corridor of the ground floor, where a row of closed doors punctuates walls covered in brown tin, the tin itself coated with soot that gleams like oil, or like the walls of a mine. At the top of the staircase is an old toilet in a closet. The ravaged floors have been partly stripped back to reveal successive layers of linoleum in a garish array of cheap patterns. A bedroom, a kitchen, and a common room for each apartment, no running water — the building is bleakly candid about the commodification of its former occupants' lives. To have had children in such cramped quarters would have inevitably meant sending them out onto the street as soon as they could walk.

I imagine it through Lansky's eyes, Lansky who came there at the age of twelve. A fight breaks out and everybody on the street scatters. Heads open up with blood. He sees them looking at each other and breathing, even as they swing with the iron bars. Three or four boys lie on the wet ground holding their faces, curled up in balls. When the gunshots start, the casings hit the street with a ring like coins. He can see them shining there.

What is it that makes him stay and watch? What is it that makes him compelled and not repulsed?

INTIFADA

It's 2001. They blow up the discotheque by the Dolphinarium in Tel Aviv. They blow up a seder in a dining room at the Park Hotel in Netanya. A year later, twenty-one teenagers die outside the discotheque, most of them the children of Soviet immigrants. In Netanya, the dead are mainly elderly people without family, some of them Holocaust survivors. A place where children can watch dolphins or go to dance parties. A hotel that offers a seder for those alone on Passover. After a while, I can't watch the TV coverage anymore — not the suicide bombings, not the bulldozers razing the refugee camps. In Tel Aviv, they are throwing stones. In Jenin, they are throwing stones. We've been through this all before, many times. My son won't return my phone calls or my e-mails. It's not a declaration, it's simply an absence, a failure to respond. I wonder what, if anything, he thinks about the war going on all around us. It's the Second Intifada and my son and I are both veering toward a state of homelessness.

PERMANENT WAR

The gangsters built their houses on pretense, hypocrisy, deception — that was the country in which they staked their claim. They owed their lavish homes and wealth to a law conceived by America's heartland Protestants, people who feared immigrants — who equated immigrants and the urban places in which they lived with sin. But of course it was Prohibition itself that urged these fears into dismal reality. The immigrants really did form criminal conspiracies, they really did corrupt judges and politicians, they really did murder people, they really did take over whole cities and become wealthy beyond their dreams.

The price of course was permanent war. On October 17, 1929, Charlie Luciano was tortured and almost killed while Meyer Lansky and his pregnant wife, Anne, were at their apartment in Brooklyn. It turned out to be the start of what would be called the Castellammarese War. Lansky's first son, Bernard, or Buddy, was born during the Castellammarese War. No one knows for certain how many people died during its two-year course.

Lansky's younger son, Paul, who would go on to graduate from West Point, went first to the prestigious Horace Mann School in the Bronx, where perhaps he first heard the word "phony."[2] The Lanskys' apartment on Central Park West was "phony." Paul's mother and her friends, the Jewish wives with their mink coats and jewels, were "phony." No doubt the Horace Mann School itself was full of "phonies." The older son, Buddy, stayed home all day — he had left school at fifteen because he'd been born with a kind of disability that no one knew what to call other than "cerebral palsy." He had trouble walking. He limped along with the contorted shuffle of an elderly woman rising from a bed. For Anne Lansky, the mother, the apartments on Central Park West — first in the Majestic, then in the Beresford — became a kind of hiding place or ward. She withdrew into eccentricity, then madness, ultimately, Robert Lacey reports in *Little Man: Meyer Lansky and the Gangster Life*, attacking her husband with a kitchen knife. They divorced in 1947, the year Bugsy Siegel was murdered in Los Angeles. Before that, Anne had escaped from a psychiatric clinic — "all the way from Riverdale in a nightgown," Lacey writes — only to collapse in front of Buddy, who, Lacey reports, would always remember "the knock on the door from the men in white coats, the protesting cries of his mother, the strange heavy jacket with the strings on the sleeves."

"Paul says everything about this place is phony," Buddy blurts and sheepishly smiles, and his father, Meyer Lansky, finds himself confronting some warped and unmanned

2. Lacey, *Little Man: Meyer Lansky and the Gangster Life*

version of himself from a long time ago. He can see his own eyes in Buddy's eyes, his own childhood self in Buddy's tentative fatuous grin. It's an immigrant's grin, the open-faced smile of the newly arrived.

CONSPIRATORS

I don't think my son Eliav even wants the power he has over me — he just has it. My ex-wife sees him from time to time, but when I ask her about his silence, she won't offer any clues. I gather that if she tells me anything it will only jeopardize her own rare contact with him. Although she never says so, I also know that in some instinctive way she blames me for his deterioration. I of course blame myself. There's no other way to feel about it, no matter what I try to tell myself.

DISCLOSURE

Towering over both of them was Salvatore Lucania who at age twenty-one had a bad reputation. Even as Lansky watched, Lucania kicked the woman in the side.

"You bitch," he shouted.

And now Lansky realized the woman was laughing through her tears.

In the fashion of Hank Messick, I'm going to make up my own version now, improvising the scenes. Call it poetic license. Call it a countermythology. Having read the books in the bibliography and looked at length at the photographs, I'm going to do what most people do, which is to imagine what isn't there.

SEPARATION

In the bedroom, Lansky opened the suitcase on top of the mound of clothes and put his laundry in the hamper, the suits in a special cloth bag. Sweaters and dresses and shoes and handbags — in his absence, Anne had left them in a pile that sloped from the bed onto the floor, probably living for a month out of that mess. He went into the bathroom, where the sink was so thickly cluttered with cosmetics bottles and shampoos and tonics and medications that he couldn't wash his hands. He took a tablet for his ulcers, swallowing it dry.

She was watching him from the doorway, her eyes swollen.

"Buddy should be home soon," she said. "He gets back four, four-thirty."

"We're going to the ballgame tomorrow. I'll see him then."

"You told me that. I forgot. You should take his friend Vince."

"Vince."

"Vince drives him to the clinic. He drives him everywhere in that little car of his. You should treat him to the game."

The gauze curtains were drawn against the sunlight. She did a certain kind of crossword puzzle that came in big cheap books made of gray paper with ink that smudged, and one of them was flopped open on the floor with a pile of quilts and blankets next to it. There were more blankets on the sofa, a pair of eyeglasses and a bottle of Bayer aspirin and a clutter of cups and saucers and the torn sleeves of soda crackers.

"I just came to get some things," he said.

"I've been feeling under the weather lately. The pollen. It's spring."

He stood there rigid in the effort of not saying anything. "I've got to go," he said. "I've got someone waiting."

He replenished the suitcase with clean shirts in cardboards, half a dozen suits, socks, underwear, ties. Then he went downstairs and drove to where he was staying that week, his sister's apartment on Ocean Parkway in Brooklyn.

DIVORCE

My wife and I divorced when our son Eliav was ten. Eighteen years later, in 2001, she gives me a birthday present, a book of the paintings of the Israeli artist Ivan Schwebel, whose work conflates time. There are pictures of King David dancing in triumph, as in the Bible, but in the background not the Judean hills but cattle cars bound for Auschwitz. There are pictures of David spying Bathsheba across a highway or from the roof of a warehouse, the setting not ancient Jerusalem but the modern city's Ben Yehuda Street or Jaffa Road or sometimes even the Bronx, barbed wire fencing off the rows of tenements. In some pictures, David looks like a grizzled man in his sixties, in others he is young, in others he is paired with a blurred figure of Jesus. In the pictures he is never at rest, never at home. At the end of the triumphant dance sequence, there are two paintings of David facing his first wife, Michal, who confronts him on a modern street at night in a scene reminiscent of a Hollywood movie, her eyes moist and accusing in the way of a betrayed woman. In the next panel, they stand like two drunks in a moment of hopeless recognition. A mugging goes on behind them in the sudden illumination of a car's headlights. He has indeed betrayed her and he will betray her further, and in the picture both he and his first wife seem to already know this.

SON

Buddy, the son, shuffled on his friend Vince's arm, his father, Meyer Lansky, trailing behind them. They made their slow way along the mezzanine in half darkness, the field appearing in bright slivers at each gate, people standing at the chute's mouth, waiting for their seats. They approached the usher, his crimped face glaring unshaven beneath a kind of gray sergeant's cap with a white bill. It occurred to Buddy that he should just tell Vince he had to go to the bathroom now, get it over with, but his father was pushing forward with the tickets — he'd had to come up with an extra one today for Vince, arguing at the Will Call desk — and he turned to Buddy and put his hand on Buddy's shoulder, his eyes full of crisis, raising his chin and saying, "This is us, we're here."

The green diamond glowed beneath him and induced a kind of vertigo as Buddy bent forward with his arms out at the side, seeking balance. The whole row had not only to stand up but to leave their seats and wait on the steps as he went awkwardly by. When he and his father and Vince finally got situated, it turned out that the Browns already had a leadoff man on first. No outs, the next batter at 1 and 0 — they had missed maybe five or six pitches, but they'd missed the first man on base. His father took a seat and looked at the field. It would not be easy for him to forget that they'd missed it. He made a note in his program. He liked to recalculate the batting averages after each hitter, interested in the game's statistics, while Buddy lost himself in the slow story of it, watching the men move in the distance from his perch in the stands. The Browns used to have a player named Pete Gray who played one-handed — he had to catch and throw with the same hand, because his right arm had been amputated as a boy after a farming accident — but now they were just a lackluster team in seventh place — *What were they doing with the leadoff man already on?* his father would be thinking — they'd been a lackluster team all Buddy's life, even Pete Gray had just been a novelty to attract fans during the war. Vince was thudding his hands together and saying *Let's go,* as if it were the sanest, most natural thing in the world, but of course Buddy knew that with his father there any use of the voice at all was a mistake. Vince, the student teacher with the little Chevrolet who must be getting some kind of course credit for being so nice to Buddy, who lived with his mother amid a pile of laundry and who spent three days a week at the clinic having his legs pressed in machines.

He watched his father watch the batter foul a pitch off

to the first-base side, the count now full. If he had to get up and go to the bathroom, he would bother everyone in the row all over again — they would all have to stand up and let him pass. How mental the body was. He felt it burning down his groin and the more he resolved not to think about it the more he knew he wouldn't last. The crowd was mostly men in hats and shirtsleeves, their ties loosened, except for an older woman in the row ahead who had a pocket mirror and tweezers and who was plucking hairs out of a mole on her face as if there were no one else there.

He told Vince he had to go to the bathroom.

His father remained still, looking at the field. At first it was as if he hadn't heard, and Buddy felt grateful, but then his father gripped the armrest of his seat and started standing up, his eyes still on the game. Vince watched him, about to speak, but then didn't. Why had Buddy assumed that Vince would take him and not his father?

REHAB

My son Eliav walks to the bus, on his way to work now like everybody else — a year later, 2002. He lives in a group home and my ex-wife says he's doing better, though he never goes anywhere without his Walkman and its tinny patter of cymbal sounds. In the cafeteria, the light is gray and the air smells of refrigerated blood. There are stock-pots as large as witches' cauldrons and mixing bowls with long wooden oars. Cooks in hats squeeze dough and frosting out of guns. Behind a pane of glass, my son can see the butchers in their red-smeared aprons working with saws, the sides of beef encased in thin white membranes and whorls of white fat.

He tells my ex-wife that he has come to live more deeply inside his own skin now, to see his mind as an obstacle or a trap, something he's learning to step around or avoid. In addition to rehab, he is mandated to work in the kitchen thirty hours a week. He says he doesn't mind the apron or the paper hat. He stands at the great stainless-steel sink, more like a series of connected counters or shallow troughs, and sprays water at dirty silverware. He separates forks, knives, and spoons and forces them into plastic canisters. He arranges the canisters on plastic crates, then he clears the muck from the draining alleys, and he walks the crates to the mouth of the dish line. Later, when the silverware is finished, he goes over to stack plates with the older men.

What he wants, he tells my ex-wife, is to apprentice himself to the dish line, the anonymity of work. He wants to develop calluses on his hands and smoke cigarettes with the Yemenite men on the loading dock who treat him with a fairness that he doesn't feel he deserves. The plates come out of the dish line so hot that only these older men can handle them, whisking them out four at a time — fast, fast — then handing them off to be stacked in the spring-loaded caddy. They hand them to my son. The plates are still so hot that he has to toss them aside almost immediately, the china taut as stone, lacquer-bright, hitting the caddy with a ring. He has to snap them four at a time from the old men's hands, and sometimes a plate slips and explodes, shattering in a thousand shards of unleashed energy and heat.

I imagine at night he rides in a friend's car with the windows open and the wind blasting tight and cold on his face. They move fast beneath the arced lights, my son's head nothing but wind and sound and the lights flicking by like small dark moons through the lenses of his sunglasses. He closes his eyes in the backseat, riding in the dark car, not thinking about anything but the feel of the motion, the sound of the air, the invulnerable feeling of distance.

HOMELAND

A place where children can watch dolphins or go to dance parties. A hotel that offers a seder for those alone on Passover. D9R armored bulldozers, painted beige like the dust, push the refugee camps into rubble. With their large blades, with the cages around their cockpits, they look mindless, like mammoth insects. The Palestinian boys throw stones. Some of them wear T-shirts, some have scarves over their faces like bandits or religious zealots. The bulldozers are impervious to the stones, impervious to bombs, machine guns, even rocket-propelled grenades. I watched it happen. I struggled against it and still don't know what I could have done differently. It took less than sixty years for my country to devolve to this, less than the span of my life.

I PITY THE POOR IMMIGRANT

THE "FAMILY"

A GENOVESE FAMILY TREE

Joe "The Boss" Masseria (1887–1931)
Sicilian-American crime boss. Killed by five bullets
at the Nuova Villa Tammaro restaurant,
Coney Island, Brooklyn, 1931.

↓

Charlie "Lucky" Luciano (1897–1962)
Founder of the current Five Families of American organized
crime. Imprisoned, 1936. Deported to Italy, 1946.

↓

Frank Costello (1891–1973)
Acting head of the Luciano crime family, 1936–1957. Retired
after being shot by Vincent "The Chin" Gigante on orders
of Vito Genovese, 1957.

↓

Vito Genovese (1897–1969)
Assumed control of the Luciano crime family under his own
name after the retirement of Frank Costello and the murder
of his other chief rival, Albert Anastasia, 1957.

* A note on the murder of Joe Masseria. The assassination took place
after a long lunch meeting between Masseria and Charlie Luciano, who
excused himself to go to the bathroom, whereupon four gunmen
entered the restaurant and opened fire. The first, Ben Siegel, was murdered in 1947. The second, Albert Anastasia, was murdered in 1957.
The third, Joe Adonis, was deported to Italy in 1956, where he died in
1971. The fourth, Vito Genovese, died in prison in 1969.

NO WAY HOME

As I said, the gangsters built their houses on pretense, hypocrisy, deception — the country in which they'd staked their claim was more like a kind of dreamland, bordered by prison, exile, and death.

On February 7, 1946, Meyer Lansky stood on the deck of the Ellis Island ferry with Frank Costello and a lawyer named Moses Polakoff, an excess of luster or glow about them even from a distance, despite their understated, impeccable clothes. They watched the Immigration Station emerge before them, the verdigris of its four turrets somehow Eastern European, circuslike, absurd. When the boat docked, they walked up the same gangway they had walked as children, Ellis Island in 1946 not a point of immigration but a point of deportation. Their friend Charlie Luciano was detained there, having spent the past ten years in Dannemora prison. They met him in the visiting room upstairs in the main building, which was eerily abandoned, its vast reception hall empty. Luciano slouched with his arms crossed over his knees, withered, pale, dressed like a custodian in gray pants and shirt. He was being sent back to the town of his birth, Lercara Friddi — some rubble on a hill in Sicily, the stink of sulfur, goats in the yellow grass. They entered the room with its big oak table and the guard closed the door, and before saying goodbye Luciano told them a story:

When they drove me through the city I asked the detectives to stop, just for a couple of minutes. I only wanted to get out and put my feet down on the street in Manhattan. I wanted to feel it under me. I wanted to know that I actually walked in New York. . . . But them guys said they couldn't allow it. So we went right on through the ferry across the bay.[3]

CRIMINOPOLIS

The destination of this journey is home. Upon arrival, we will find, as we might have expected, that home is no longer there.

Meyer Lansky, Bugsy Siegel, Lucky Luciano. If I told you there was a parallel to be drawn between their founding of Las Vegas and the dream of Israel, would you give me enough time to explain? It first occurs to me in 2006. A visiting poet in a city not known for poetry, I am determined on my first visit to Las Vegas not to find the cliché that I expect, and perhaps for that reason I find something else. There is a university — that's why I've come, to read at the Black Mountain Institute of the University of Nevada, Las Vegas. Its urban campus spreads out in concrete, stone, glass, and palm trees in a way that can't help but remind me of the universities in Tel Aviv, Jerusalem, Haifa. I am staying not downtown but on the Strip, at the Bellagio with its famous fountains. The spectacle is at first disorienting, then lulling. Everything is brightly colored but the ambient sound, especially in the casinos, is hushed, a function of the rooms' enormous size, the sound like gamelan music heard across a wide valley. I go for a long walk on the Strip one

---

3. Gosch, *The Last Testament of Lucky Luciano*

morning. There's a point beyond the New York-New York Hotel and Casino where the massive resorts peter out and you see the illusion wither, the Strip just a road in the desert, a few convenience stores with slot machines and gas pumps. But that is what I expected to find. What I did not expect to find was the sheer scale of the Bellagio, the Paris, the MGM Grand, the Venetian. I did not expect the daydream to be so available and expansive and real. What I did not expect, above all, was that I would want to stay there.

PROMISED LAND

It was a harrowing journey. The temperature rose to 120 degrees, the wires in their Cadillac melting. "There were times when I thought I would die in that desert," Lansky said. "Vegas was a horrible place, really just a small oasis town."

— **Sally Denton and Roger Morris**, *The Money and the Power: The Making of Las Vegas and Its Hold on America, 1947–2000*

Lansky and Ben Siegel saw it first from the highway at a distance, then closer, the angles changing, different contours and shadows revealing themselves, the hotel and its casino a massive abandoned hall standing with its wings at a diagonal to the road, set far back on cleared ground that had been scooped and plowed into berms, cut with sewage canals, scored with the wide tread of bulldozers. The half-finished Flamingo seemed already to have become a ruin of itself, as if they were viewing it not now but a thousand years from now. The work had stopped and so there were no people around, no trucks or heavy equipment, their only traces some deserted sheds and utility buildings and a few wooden power poles powdered with dust.

"I think you should come out here and keep an eye on it," Lansky said.

Siegel turned to him with a half smile that was already fading and pointed out the emptiness of where they were.

DEFINITION

immigrate *vi.* to come into a new country, region or environment, esp. in order to settle there, as in the newborn entering the world, consciousness entering the brain, the corpse returning to the earth, silence on either side of the transit.

FOUNDING FATHER

"The Man Who Invented Las Vegas," according to the book by that title written by the man's son, W. R. Wilkerson III, was not Meyer Lansky or Ben Siegel but a publisher and restaurateur named Billy Wilkerson. Wilkerson had made his fortune from the famous newspaper he'd founded, the *Hollywood Reporter,* and then from a group of restaurants, including the iconic Ciro's, in Beverly Hills. There is a photograph of Billy Wilkerson with Ben Siegel at Wilkerson's Los Angeles barbershop and haberdashery, the Sunset House, where, Wilkerson III writes, Siegel enjoyed "close personal ties with the shop's main barber, Harry

Drucker," who "always made sure that Siegel got the best shave, facial, haircut and manicure of the day." In the photograph, Billy Wilkerson has a mustache like the actor William Powell's. He liked French poodles and days at the track alone in the box with binoculars and cigarettes, a silk handkerchief in his jacket pocket. In February of 1945, he bought thirty-three acres of land outside of Las Vegas on what would eventually be called "the Strip," and there began the construction of the casino and hotel he was going to call the Flamingo Club. It was going to be a new kind of casino for Las Vegas, modeled after Monte Carlo, with a dress code that would require black tie for men. It would be the first hotel in the United States to have central air-conditioning. In the casino, there would be no windows, no clocks, no way of knowing what time it was, just an unchanging half-light in which to get lost. Like some secret world behind a door in a dream, the casino would spin out a vision of opulence so potent in its details — the ebony-colored matchbook with the pink Flamingo emblem at its center — that you would miss it keenly if it weren't for the knowledge that you could always go back. Wilkerson knew it would succeed, because he himself was a chronic gambler. He frequently lost twenty-five thousand dollars in a single day. This was why he wanted to build the Flamingo, because he thought that if he owned the house, he couldn't lose.

His son writes that construction of the Flamingo began in November of 1945 and that "nearly a third" of the hotel and casino were completed by the time Wilkerson ran into financial problems two months later, in January 1946. Wilkerson gambled $150,000 of his remaining $200,000 and lost all of it. "A businessman from the east coast," G. Harry Rothberg, learned of this predicament and offered to help, Wilkerson III recounts. G. Harry Rothberg was in fact a front for Meyer Lansky, whom Billy Wilkerson would never meet and whose connection to Rothberg he may have never known.

A month later, two other Lansky associates, Moe Sedway and Gus Greenbaum, came to visit the construction site to check on Wilkerson's progress. "They brought with them a loudly-dressed character who enthusiastically presented himself to the publisher as his new partner," Wilkerson III writes. "This man was Ben Siegel," who was no longer just Wilkerson's colorful acquaintance but now the co-manager of his hotel and casino.

STATELESS

It was legal — Las Vegas was like Cuba in this way. Among other things, Las Vegas and Cuba would have seemed like safe havens, places of refuge. They all would have seen that the same thing that had just happened to Luciano could happen to any of them. At any time they could be sent to jail or back where they'd come from.

In September of 1946, Lansky sent Luciano a telegram in Sicily that said, "December — Hotel Nacional." It meant they were to meet in Havana at that time. The plan was for Luciano's exile to take place not in Italy but in Havana, just a short plane or boat ride away from the U.S., the only place he had ever felt at home.

From Cuban author Enrique Cirules, T. J. English passes on to us this portrait of the first night of the "Havana

Conference," which reunited Lansky with Luciano and their cohort of Jewish and Italian gangsters, the uneasy alliance of men who had invested millions in the casinos of Las Vegas and Cuba:

> There were crab and queen conch enchiladas brought from the southern archipelago. For the main course, there was a choice of roast breast of flamingo, tortoise stew, roast tortoise with lemon and garlic, and crayfish, oysters, and grilled swordfish from the nearby fishing village of Cojímar. There was also grilled venison sent by a government minister from Camagüey who owned livestock and, the most obscure delicacy of all, grilled manatee. The guests drank *añejo* rum and smoked Montecristo cigars.
>
> Later, the visiting delegates were encouraged to make the most of their inaugural night in Havana. A fleet of fifty cars with chauffeurs was at the ready. Dancers and showgirls from the city's three main nightclubs — the Tropicana, the Montmartre, and the Sans Souci — were selected and paid for their services, as were prostitutes from Casa Marina, the classiest and most renowned bordello in the city.

One reads this passage and fails to connect it in any way to what one knows about the silent, inward Lansky. What would he have ordered from that preposterous menu? What would he have done after dinner but gone to his room?

It's finally quiet when the girl arrives, only a faint sound of music coming in through the partly opened window.

She's young and speaks no English, and he makes her a drink with a cube of ice from the bucket and they sit on the bed in the dim light and he looks down at his hands. After a while, he touches her chin and slowly turns her face and looks at her with something like mild rebuke or even pain in his eyes. He takes her glass back in his hands and she stands up and turns away and steps out of her shoes, then she reaches behind her for the zipper of her dress.

CLASS

"Class, that's the only thing that counts in life. Class. Without class and style a man's a bum, he might as well be dead."

— Ben Siegel

Ben Siegel, son of Ukrainian peasants, could now look at a room and see what was really there — what kind of marble was on the floor, if the drapes were silk or gabardine. He could discern these subtle differences, or at least he told people he could.

He had once watched Billy Wilkerson speaking to Cary Grant and some blond tomboyish starlet in a picture hat, and it had been the movie star who was trying to charm Wilkerson, not the other way around, the actor holding an invisible box in his hands to signal the joke, Wilkerson in his cream-colored suit already smiling, his knuckle raised impatiently to rap the table in response. Night after night, Billy Wilkerson would move from table to table in his Beverly Hills restaurants — Ciro's, Café Trocadero — crouching for five or ten minutes at a stretch rather than pulling up a chair, always smoking, offering some strong opinion about who was going to do what next and who was finished. He never ate before midnight and even then he just cut into his steak to assess how done it was, maybe taking a few bites with a glass of gin. He never quoted movies or told set jokes and when he used profanity, which was seldom, it was dirtier than anyone else's.

"As time went on," Wilkerson III writes of his father's relationship with his partner Ben Siegel, "the gangster's respectful admiration disintegrated into an insane, all-consuming jealousy."

Arguments between the ostensible partners escalated. Siegel and his mistress, an ex-dancer named Virginia Hill, began revising the plans — building, tearing down, rebuilding, each time with more extravagance. Every bathroom in the guest suites was fitted with its own "private plumbing and sewer system. Cost: $1,150,000," Wilkerson III writes.

"This is my fucking hotel," Siegel is quoted as saying to the journalist Westbrook Pegler. "My idea! Wilkerson has nothing to do with it!"

In fear of his life, Billy Wilkerson finally fled to Paris. He "rarely went outside," his son comments. "Every Sunday, he made a single major excursion. He took a cab to Mass at Notre Dame Cathedral."

STYLE

Anne Lansky in photographs is sometimes dreamy, leaning forward with a nearly finished cigarette between her fingertips, dressed like an actress in a tailored suit with white fleece collar and cuffs, a string of pearls, a corsage made from a large flower, perhaps a chrysanthemum. But even in those expensive clothes, her accent would have given her away. There would have been signs of wrongness, signs that she could only guess at but never fully perceive because she herself was distorted.

AMOUR FOU

From the roof of his new palace, David first encounters Bathsheba. *And it happened at eventide that David arose from his bed and walked about on the roof of the king's house, and he saw from the roof a woman bathing, and the woman was very beautiful.*

He'd been dozing all that afternoon and perhaps he was as naked as she was when he traipsed outdoors in the fading light and saw her there.

FAREWELL

It was evening and Ben wore a dark suit and a dark tie and he had showered recently enough that his hair was still a little damp at the sideburns. He lit a match whose gold tip slowly erupted in a flame so high he had to hold it away from his body. His hair was not only damp, Meyer saw, but starting to thin a little. He reached the ashtray toward him and inhaled.

"You're still with Anne," Ben said. "Still married."

"She's ill. You know that."

"I'm just saying you should think of yourself a little."

"Like you."

Though still unfinished, the Flamingo was two million dollars over budget. You wondered how Ben could put himself in such a position, and then you remembered that his whole life was full of mistakes and embarrassments that he endured out of necessity and then forgot.

"I came out here because you asked me to," he said. "I got invested in it, I don't know why. All the details."

"It seems like you've had a lot of fun ideas out here."

"Don't give me that look. The sad shtetl in that look."

Virginia came in holding a bottle of Coca-Cola with a long straw tilting out of its neck. She had pushed her sunglasses back over the front roll of her hair — without the sunglasses her eyes were hazel and without mystery. She handed the bottle to Ben and he put it down on the desk and spread his arms, and she hesitated for a moment, as if about to come sit in his lap, but then she turned and left the room without ever quite looking at Meyer. Maybe the lack of refinement and depth made her sexy in a frank, resolute way. Maybe he saw it and it made him like her less each time he was with her. You left someone in a different part of the world, even for just a year, and he changed in so many ways that you could only mourn the loss. It was that the new place brought out what had always been latent inside him. Distance revealed his flaws.

THE OLD COUNTRY

Safe havens, places of refuge. Of course in Lansky's case there was no such analogy as Lercara Friddi — there was no place to be sent back to. The place he had come from had disappeared, become *judenrein*. They'd taken his part of Grodno and deported it to Auschwitz and Treblinka.

BASEBALL

Buddy Lansky was at his usual table with the sports pages when the woman sat down across from him, her shoulders slanted a little to one side. His friend Sam had been watching from the bar, but when she came over Sam walked back toward his office. The woman wore dark lipstick and had faint wrinkles at the corners of her eyes, the collar of her yellow blouse jutting out over the lapel of her jacket. Not drunk, but drinking. The electric fans rattling in their cages at the corners of the room. She told him her name and he was about to tell her his, but she would have known, he was sure, there was no point. He looked back down at the blurred league standings, anchored there with the side of his swollen hand. The waiter brought the woman a beer and asked Buddy if he wanted anything and Buddy said no, he was fine. He went there almost every day — everyone knew whose son he was. Sometimes they played cards, sometimes he just listened to them talk.

"You're not very good at this, are you?" the woman said.

"Good at what?"

"Good at chatting people up. Making them feel at ease. Letting them know what you want."

She brought two fingers and her thumb to her glass of beer, then took a meditative sip, barely tipping the glass, holding it in that delicate way, but when she put it down, it hit the table harder than she expected.

"A baseball fan," she said. "Isn't that funny? I never understood a thing about baseball."

She extended her hand across the table, a lazy form of beckoning, waiting for him to understand: he was supposed to clasp it. It was a dry, slender hand, the insides of the fingers lined and creased, but it was long, well formed. Her age was terrifying and alluring at the same time. Sam had made him a standing offer of the use of his apartment. That was the joke Sam always made.

They took a cab across town. At the entrance to the cement-fronted building on Lexington Avenue, a doorman stood inside the opened glass, nothing on his face. He mentioned the apartment number and gave Buddy an envelope with the key, and Buddy and the woman took the elevator to the fifth floor, not talking anymore. There were some old chairs and a yellow cloth couch and a radio, a kitchenette off to the side. She poured herself a drink at the little makeshift bar and Buddy stood there looking out the windows at the white sunlight between the buildings.

"We'll just take it easy," she said. "Go ahead and lie down. Do you like music or is it just baseball? I used to sing, believe it or not. Lee Sherman's band. What I liked best, though, was to sing with just a piano, that intimacy. I never had a big voice. I wasn't good for singing with a band."

She switched on the radio, an ad for Lux soap, then she reached back and took the pins out of her hair, shaking it loose. She took off her jacket, then her blouse. He didn't experience any of this as quite real. Not the sight of her in her brassiere, nor the sight of her stepping out of her heels and taking off her skirt. The brassiere and the girdle left lines in her flesh, and the sheer black stockings made her hips and thighs seem unusually broad. When she sat next to him, he was overwhelmed by the sudden fact of her warmth, the air she exhaled, the thin gold strand around her neck. Her touch made it clearer. The hard fact of her experience made it clearer. He tried to kiss her and she moved away with such professional skill that he felt his body recede into vagueness. She took off the brassiere, reaching behind her back for the clasp like an athletic girl, one foot tucked behind her on the couch. He saw her breasts swing free and for a minute or two he was no longer Buddy.

DECLINE AND FALL

On December 26, 1946, the still-unfinished Flamingo had its disastrous grand opening with Xavier Cugat and His Orchestra, Jimmy Durante, Rose Marie, and a few other entertainers playing to a half-empty room of mostly local Nevadans in ranch clothes. Robert Lacey recounts:

> There were no bedrooms for guests. So on the night the Flamingo opened for business, it was the neighboring El Rancho Las Vegas and the Last Frontier which made the big money, as the guests from the Flamingo's opening reception came back to their hotels, sent

their wives off to bed, and decided to play for an hour or so with the winnings they had brought from the new casino down the road.

The same pattern continued through the entire Christmas week of 1946 and through the New Year's celebrations of 1947....Late in January 1947, the new Flamingo Hotel Casino closed its doors, less than a month after it had opened.

The week before this failed grand opening, Charlie Luciano's lieutenant, Vito Genovese, had arrived at the Havana Conference four days early, as if already smelling blood. Genovese had been hiding in Italy, where during the war he'd allied himself with Benito Mussolini and begun smuggling narcotics. Before that, Genovese had murdered many people, including Joe "The Boss" Masseria, with the help of Luciano, Ben Siegel, Albert Anastasia, and Joe Adonis, all of whom, like Genovese, were now investors in Siegel and Lansky's unfinished Flamingo. On the night of the failed grand opening, after the bad news came via a phone call from Las Vegas, Genovese demanded to speak in private with Luciano at their hotel in Havana. Luciano, via his biographer Martin Gosch, is made to recount the episode in *The Last Testament of Lucky Luciano:*

Naturally, we was pretty damn depressed about what happened in Vegas, and nobody felt like talkin' much to nobody else that night. By this time it was four o'clock in the mornin'. I started to leave, but Vito stopped me and asked could I come up to his suite on the top floor. . . . Just as sure as I was alive it meant that Vito had tipped off Washington about my bein' in Havana and probably made it sound like I was handlin' junk. . . . So I done somethin' that I never done before, and it was against all the rules that I myself set up. I pushed him up against the wall and I beat the livin' daylights out of him. . . . I didn't hit him in the face — I didn't want to mark him up. I just belted him in the guts and in the kidneys, and when he fell down I just started to kick him in the belly. . . . I beat him up so bad he couldn't get out of his room for three days.

But the coup had begun, Vito Genovese's coup. The Havana Conference had hardly been discreet — the fleet of fifty cars with chauffeurs at the ready, the dancers and showgirls and prostitutes from Casa Marina. The U.S. had indeed been tipped off that Luciano was in Cuba, and soon, bowing to American pressure, Batista's government would deport Luciano back to Italy, where he would eventually die. His fall, along with Ben Siegel's murder that June, would leave Lansky defenseless.

"When I walk the streets," Lansky would later tell an FBI agent, "I never know when I might get it." Robert Lacey writes, "There were too many 'nuts' running around — and, Meyer noted, 'he no longer has friends he can trust among the Italians.'"

The Luciano family had become the Genovese family. What Vito Genovese started, Fidel Castro would continue later when he nationalized Cuba's casinos. "His troops smashed hundreds of slot machines, dice and roulette tables and other gaming devices in the Havana tourist hotels," the *New York Times* wrote in their obituary of Lansky. Castro's revolution "ended a multi-million-dollar industry and Mr. Lansky's substantial interests in it." He never recovered from these multi-million-dollar losses.

It turned out there were no safe havens, no places of refuge.

From the flyleaf of Hank Messick's 1971 biography:

LANSKY owns some of the Bahamas, more of Las Vegas and most of Miami.

LANSKY has a personal fortune of $300,000,000.

LANSKY has beaten six murder charges and survived many of his closest associates — Bugsy Siegel, Lucky Luciano, Fulgencio Batista.

LANSKY is the mystery man behind organized crime in America.

These are some of the myths that chased him out of Israel.

TABLOID

Safe havens, places of refuge. Places willing to accept even people like them — Meyer Lansky, Bugsy Siegel, Lucky Luciano.

On June 20, 1947, Ben Siegel arrived at the Sunset House in Beverly Hills on the morning of his murder and presumably got the best shave, facial, haircut, and manicure of the day from the head barber, Harry Drucker. The hotel at the Flamingo was finally completed. It had reopened and by June, six months after its closing, it had even begun turning a profit. Siegel went with a friend named Alan Smiley to his mistress Virginia Hill's house on North Linden Drive, where upstairs Hill's brother Chris was in one of the bedrooms with his girlfriend. In photographs you can see a bronze figurine of a dancing girl on the coffee table in the living room where Siegel and Smiley sat, Siegel reading the *Los Angeles Times*, Smiley perhaps sharing it with him. No one has ever offered an explanation of the casually strange assortment of people in that house — the lovers upstairs, the two men idly wasting time below. Virginia Hill wasn't there. She was in Paris. "The assassin was found to have rested the carbine on the lattice-work of a rose-covered pergola just outside the window," Lacey writes, "close enough to smash in Benny's left eye, crush the bridge of his nose, and shatter a vertebra at the back of his neck. His right eye was blown out completely, and was later found fifteen feet away from his body."

In his book on his father, Billy Wilkerson, W. R. Wilkerson III presents a photograph of an invitation to the Flamingo's grand opening and writes:

> ... Siegel's underlings had finally summoned the courage to tell their boss that all the matchbooks cited Wilkerson as the manager. In Las Vegas, "managers" were also proprietors and owners. Thousands of these books had been printed. In a rage, Siegel ordered everything with Wilkerson's name on it destroyed. Because there wasn't enough time to reprint the matchbooks, some brave soul suggested a number be saved for the opening. Siegel hired a squad of women with black grease pencils to strike out the publisher's name wherever it appeared.

Wilkerson III provides photographs of the matchbooks. Of his father, he writes, "He is the quintessential victim of myth.... For three decades, practically everyone in Hollywood knew him, or of him. Yet a mere thirty years after his death Billy Wilkerson is practically unknown."

His name was not on the matchbooks. In a sense, you could say that Ben Siegel was murdered by his fellow gangsters because he cared too much about whose name was on the matchbooks.

DIASPORA

Meyer woke up thinking he was in Florida, but gradually realizing he didn't know where he was — he could feel the orientation of the room except that everything was backwards, the door to his left instead of his right, the hallway behind him instead of in front. It was very dark and he lay there for a long time in thick half-sleep, anxious, still not knowing. His stomach burned and swelled like a drum beneath the muscle. It burned all the way to his throat, which was raw as if from screaming. He wanted to switch on the lamp and take something, but it was hard to move in the dark, so he lay there. He sometimes thought of words in Polish or Yiddish and couldn't remember them. *Żołądek. Żołądek podchodził mi do gardła. S'tut vey der mogen. My stomach hurts.* He thought he was at his sister's apartment — Brooklyn, Ocean Parkway. He was on Hibiscus Drive in Hallandale, Florida. He was on Central Park West, in Kansas City, Atlantic City, Key West. He didn't know where he was. His stomach was turning to acid inside him.

I PITY THE POOR IMMIGRANT

KING

And on the pedestal these words appear:
"My name is Ozymandias, King of Kings;
Look on my works ye mighty and despair!"
Nothing beside remains. Round the decay
Of that colossal wreck, boundless and bare
The lone and level sands stretch far away.

HIGH AGAIN

The bag is gone and my son Eliav is feeling crazy now, a burning pain in his knee from all the walking he's done, trying to get somewhere, following the broken sidewalk past the men in their huddled groups, laughing at something, perhaps laughing at him. He's trying to get across town to meet his friend at some spot near the bus station, but he is higher than he'd thought, throat dry with the need for heroin, cocaine, all the marijuana in the world not enough to relax, burning his fingers on the lighter. He's walked maybe four miles by now and there's no more cigarettes, no more drugs, the street rising and dipping beneath him, and he's trying not to think about it, focused to the point of perplexity, everything swirling in at him at once, his face and hands covered in grime, the same clothes he's had on for two days. He crosses beneath the viaduct and heads for the vacant lot, cars sliding above him along the globe's groove, cars arcing back toward him down the bend, curved arcs of silver and blue. He remembers something about a sign that says PAZ — blue letters on a yellow background, PAZ — but what he no longer knows is if this sign was part of his friend's directions or whether its vivid colors and letters have only made it seem that it was part of those directions. He keeps walking down the broken pavement, faster now, looking at the sign glowing there significantly past the chain-link fence, yellow and blue, yellow and blue, then fading into a small dirty piece of tin with painted letters: PAZ. He gets himself through the hole in the chain-link fence, then starts across the vacant lot, thinking that this is right, this is what his friend had said — PAZ — prisms of light coming at him from all sides now, dust everywhere, bricks beneath his feet, a yard full of weeds. They are pale green stalks with bulging sacs beneath their flower parts, monstrous weeds velveted with tiny white hairs, and he can feel his heart pounding, a bruised ache behind the bulbs of his closed eyes, and he isn't sure anymore if this is the right vacant lot, and then in a terrible moment he is absolutely certain that his friend had never said anything about PAZ or a vacant lot at all.

ILLEGAL IMMIGRANTS

The drugs come into Israel from Lebanon — marijuana, hashish, heroin — most of the supply originating in Afghanistan, though some of it in Iraq or Turkey or in Lebanon itself. As a go-between, Hezbollah takes its cut and uses the money in its ongoing terror campaign against

Israel. Once the drugs cross the border into the Golan Heights, they are funneled through a network of Israeli crime families where ultimately there is an invisible bridge between Arab and Jew. I saw some of the Jewish side growing up. Their earliest forerunners started in the black market in the first years after Independence, when food and everyday staples were scarce — bread, milk, cigarettes. In a nation of immigrants, they were war profiteers who later branched out into other illegal businesses. I used to be fascinated by the secret money kept hidden in its envelope beneath my father's cash register. I used to be fascinated by the unfriendly boys who came each week to collect it. I was attracted and not repulsed. Everything I've learned since has taught me how false this romance is, but the romance still exists. Frequently it seems that the romance steers the world.

QED

At the Flamingo Hotel and Casino, there's a plaque commemorating Bugsy Siegel, whose "original" structure, as the text describes it, stood from December 26, 1946, until December 14, 1993.

Of course we know this is a myth — we know the hotel was Billy Wilkerson's idea, that the Flamingo was stolen from him. Of course it doesn't matter that we know this. It's a fact that has no traction, in a place that has no memory.

THIEF

My son Eliav's new girlfriend lives in a room with two folding chairs, some bedding on the floor, a naked sink jutting out of the wall, its porcelain surface rusted almost black in spots. When she answers the door, she wears a faded nightgown and a pair of old track shoes, a kerchief on her head. I offer to take her to a café but she says no, she can't leave, what if he comes back? I realize she's more concerned for my son's safety than for hers. He has taken her money and disappeared, but he still has this power over her. The dark, bruised shadows that surround her eyes are not bruises but something more like a symptom of their shared illness.

I look for causes. For example, I sent him to a university in the United States. Before that, he traveled in Asia for a year. Before that, he served thirty-six months in the intelligence division of the IDF. But it was only after he came back to Tel Aviv from all this that he disappeared.

VCR

I need to work on new poems but I can't find anything that holds my attention. It's 2004 and the fighting is general now — suicide bombings and rocket attacks on Israel, targeted assassinations and armored raids on Gaza and the West Bank. Operation Rainbow, Operation Days of Penitence — dead children, dead civilians, dead soldiers, dead terrorists. I can't lie, I have nothing new to say about it. Perhaps that's what my son is saying. I eat a dinner of bread, cucumbers, tomatoes, lime, some salt whose individual grains are so coarse I can taste them. A glass of Goldstar beer, some music. I listen to the music while I do the dishes and it mitigates my dread and the fact that I'm alone. At night, I watch gangster movies — *The Godfather, The Godfather, Part II, Goodfellas, Scarface.* They somehow calm me, soothe me. I can't explain it.

INHERITANCE

With no one to pay his bills, and with only his disability pension, Buddy Lansky was evicted from Arch Creek [a convalescent home]. His belongings — one battered suitcase, a few plastic bags of clothing, and an old television set — were packed up, and he was transported to a broken-down corner of North Miami that was noted for its tattoo parlors and for the thick wire mesh on storefront windows....

"The basic trouble," he said, looking calmly at his grubby and depressing surroundings, "is that I have lived too long."

— **Robert Lacey,** *Little Man: Meyer Lansky and the Gangster Life*

MOTEL, 1979

Divorced, alone, Buddy Lansky was forty-nine, destined for a convalescent home called Arch Creek from which he would be evicted, but for now still here at the motel.

When he woke up, the sunlight moved like pale, almost invisible clouds behind the pulled blind and he knew without looking at the clock that it was not even seven yet. He liked to sleep with the TV on, the sound turned off, sometimes not only at night but throughout the day and it was for this reason that he sometimes woke too early, like now, because he'd slept too much in the daytime. It would be at least two hours before his helper, Booker, came to undress him, the bathtub running, Booker taking the diaper off, not talking, spreading the two white towels on the bed and turning Buddy over with a low *all right,* Buddy's naked body exposed like a baby's, legs like spindled sticks, the cold air-conditioned air between his thighs. On TV there would be a game show, or there would be Dick Butkus and Bubba Smith playing golf, and Booker wouldn't seem to notice or even hear it, and sometimes the incongruity of it would make Buddy giggle nervously, and that made Booker even more silent, made it easier for Booker to say later that it would be more money next week, not just the seventy but seventy-five. The motel was all the way up in North Miami Beach near Sunny Isles, a half hour from Booker's uncle's house in Overtown, and if he couldn't borrow his uncle's car then it was at least an hour and a half by a combination of buses. They had met here at the motel, a run-down place of fake tiki roofs and rampant banana trees fronting the traffic, Booker a porter, Buddy working the switchboard there for years, until a few weeks ago when he'd begun losing the sensation in his fingers.

He lay flat in bed feeling damp, unable to move his arm for now, waiting for it to come back when he got the cir-

culation going. With just one arm, he had trouble adjust-
ing the twisted neck of his pajama shirt, and his breathing
tightened, the perspiration rising on his face. The room
smelled like cigarettes — all the rooms smelled like cigarettes and lemon disinfectant. He closed his eyes and
tried to sleep again, but his mind kept wisecracking along.
You got so bored with your despondency. The boredom
somehow called for further abasement, as if abasement
could release you from the fear. He let himself urinate
into the diaper and felt it spread over his testicles and
down his legs. He was a boy, his ex-wife Annette would
always tell him. The gambling, the prostitutes — somehow even these mistakes remained the mistakes of a boy.
He tried to go back to sleep. Then he struggled to hoist
himself into the chair that Booker had left by the bed last
night. He fisted his hands on either side of his hips and
pressed hard down into the bed and made an effort to
swivel his legs around, but he started sweating again, suddenly very hot the moment he realized he wasn't going to
do it, his brow tense, the sweat running down his face,
down his neck. It was really very funny if you thought
about it for even a minute. The wheelchair had a little
lever you pressed to make it move forward, make it move
back, but now he couldn't even do that, now the ridiculous stillness had spread farther out — arms and legs drifting free of the brain, the tide seeping up, always so slowly
that you thought it might have stopped, but it never
stopped, it had a patient sense of humor. You went from
being unable to walk to being unable to move practically
at all. They should wheel him off a bridge. Wheel him out
of an airplane. He liked the cartoon image of himself

laughing his embarrassed laugh as Booker wheeled him off the roof of the motel, the hysterical yodel of his scream, then *Crash! Bang! Whop!* He lay there daydreaming about it, then waiting for Booker to arrive, then waiting for *The Price Is Right* to start. Fifty dollars a day — that was what he was going to have to ask his father for. Not just seventy or seventy-five a week, but fifty a day. Three hundred and fifty a week. Eighteen thousand a year. That was the going rate for a full-time medical aide who could feed you and clothe you and bathe you when you could no longer do these things yourself.

COLLINS AVENUE

His father was out when they arrived, so they sat in the kitchenette, Buddy inclined in the wheelchair with his head back so that Booker could feed him, a bird with its chick, Booker cutting the peanut butter sandwich into little triangles and forking them into the chick's upturned mouth. His stepmother, Teddy, stood watching curiously at the counter as she told Buddy the kind of story she liked to tell, a story about a friend's daughter who had recurring fibroids. The story grew increasingly morbid. It was almost gratifying to hear it with Booker there, a kind of triumph to have Booker witness it, to see that she was really like this. Her friend's daughter was thirty-nine, Teddy was saying, and had never had children. Suddenly at age thirty-nine, after a first surgery had failed to cure her, her fibroids returned — "very, very serious," Teddy said — and they'd had to give the friend's daughter a total hysterectomy. It made her so despondent that she'd stopped going out, could hardly even go to work. Then the daughter's close friend got pregnant and she decided she would try to help her plan a baby shower. The friend's pregnancy brought the sick woman out of her despair for a while. She bought decorations and special paper plates and matching plastic silverware and she arranged for the caterers to bring platters of different kinds of sandwiches and a carrot cake, her friend's favorite. All this planning and decorating helped her forget about her hysterectomy, helped her feel alive again, but then on the day of the shower, just when everything was going so well, the reality of it all hit her again. She drove to her friend's house with her nicely wrapped gift and realized she couldn't go in. She just stood outside the door for a minute and then turned around and got back into the car.

"She couldn't face it," Teddy told them. "It just broke her heart. What got to her was that she'd never had any children of her own."

Booker cut the last of the sandwich into two little pieces and brought one on the fork to Buddy's mouth. *What got to her was that she'd never had any children of her own.* Of course Buddy had no children of his own either. Of course that was what his stepmother was telling him. She was telling him that he was so obtuse that he'd never even realized that the one basic truth in life was children.

CAREGIVER

"She didn't like me in her kitchen," Booker said.

Buddy grimaced and closed his eyes while Booker wiped his face roughly with the wet cloth. "She doesn't like me in it either," he said.

"How long they been married?"

"Thirty years. It was secret for a while. He kept it secret for about two years."

"Why?"

"Why not? That was more the thinking."

AUDIENCE

His father was waiting by the pool, sitting at an umbrella table by himself with a folded newspaper in the oval of shade. Booker wheeled him out and Buddy did his best to sit up straight, hands dead in his lap, glad that at least now he was thin and not pudgy, not so coddled looking. He wore a blue blazer in the summer heat. His father wore a golf shirt and pale cotton slacks. He had lost all the color in his face and his hair was gray but still thick, still slicked back in the pompadour, his eyebrows full. He didn't say anything when Buddy introduced Booker. There was all kinds of awkward clatter around the table, and then his father insisted that they sit somewhere else, beneath the veranda where Buddy would be out of the sun, and they made their way over there slowly, Buddy soaking wet beneath his clothes now, his breathing tight. You could feel your skin, you could feel the sweat, even feel the muscle and bone beneath the skin, but you couldn't move any of it. It was the same as the embarrassed grin that always came to his face. Like the embarrassed grin, the stillness was involuntary but also seemed the truest possible reflection of who he was.

"Teddy will bring out something for us to drink," his father said. "You didn't have to wear a jacket. You know that."

"I wanted to make the effort."

"It's July."

"Where is everyone? Where's the gang?"

"It's hot out. They're inside. I just came out to get some fresh air."

His father looked off far into the distance, breathing in and out slowly. The way he breathed, it was as if it hurt him in various, small increments. The pupils of his eyes had contracted into two black disks that gave him a helpless, even sightless look at times. He didn't seem to know what to do with his hands since he'd quit smoking.

Buddy craned his head up and back to try to catch Booker's eye, but he couldn't manage it, so instead he gave his sheepish laugh. Now that he'd come dressed in slacks and a blazer, he felt the same stilted discomfort he'd felt when he was ten years old and made to sit for a photograph in such clothes. He heard Booker's shoes scuffing softly away on the concrete. Don't say anything. Don't say that you're fine either. Just stick to the practical issue, the fifty dollars a day for your basic needs.

"The drinks," his father said. "How are you going to manage?"

"I'm not thirsty," Buddy said.

"You need to stay hydrated. What's his name?"

"Booker."

"Booker. We'll get him to come back to the pool. Teddy will send him back."

RIVIERA

The iced teas sat in their condensation puddles on the white fiberglass table, neither of them drinking, Booker not coming back. There was a feeling of being suspended in time, lulled by the heat and the rilled water of the unused pool. He remembered his father's penthouse in the Havana Riviera, doves outside on the balcony, his father standing there at the window in his black tuxedo, the view of the Malecón. At dusk, there would be a special intensity of gray light, a kind of anticipation of what would unfold that evening, each evening like the one before it, the waves breaking on the jetty. The fountain with its seahorse shapes, the lobby with its low-slung chairs, the women in white gloves, men in dinner jackets. Even on the top floor, you would feel the vastness of the spaces below — the casino, the Copa Bar — the city's lights outside the window, the traffic passing before night fell. He remembered they'd had a talk in the dim light about his new fiancée, Annette, and Buddy had explained that she was the right one, as if his father would understand at last and give him his blessing.

WOLF AND LAMB

His father was hardly listening to what he was saying now. What was terrifying and new for Buddy to present was turning out to be just more of the same story for his father. He knew that his father was thinking of the gambling — the gambling would always be with them now. To be his father's son and to have fallen prey to gambling — the perverse humor of that mistake would never go away. To bet on luck and whim, without skill — to know nothing of handicapping or probability or statistics. To write bad checks to cover the debts, as if the numbers in the statement were just dreams you could make disappear by not looking at them. Twelve thousand dollars in jai alai debts he'd tried to pay off from a bank account his father had set up for him, as if his father wouldn't notice, the plan so vaporous he decided to withdraw even more, a little extra to take Annette out to dinner that night, stone crabs and prime rib, then to a club to see Jackie Mason. Married to Annette, stepfather to Annette's son, presumably an adult, a family man — the humiliation of being that defective had become his core, even all these years later. He could mount an argument now — I need fifteen hundred a month because I can't take care of myself anymore — but the argument lacked force because he had long ago destroyed all his credibility, destroyed it over a lifetime of folly. To look back on the past was to understand that he had never once seen anything for what it was — even his suicide attempt was just a scene from a movie melodrama. Wake up and take yourself seriously. But he had never been able to do that. He had moved with all earnestness through a daydream without even knowing it, ever since he was born, because he was made that way, just as his father was made the other way.

THE PITCH

"They're going to let me keep the room, but there won't be any more paychecks coming," he said. "I can't do the work the way I am now. I can barely move my fingers sometimes. When it's like that, I can't move the chair."

His father wasn't looking at him. He seemed to pause, weighing his words, but then it became clear that he wasn't pausing — he was just letting Buddy's words sit there bare of consolation, as if after all these years he had finally decided to stop telling his son comforting lies. Buddy saw himself from a great distance then, wilting in the white sun with his thin legs at an angle, polished black shoes on the footrests. He wondered if his father had been testing him in this heat on purpose. *Never take your jacket off,* he used to say. *If you're hot, then calm down.* He looked at the shiny brass buttons on the cuff of his blazer. The failed marriage, the aimlessness, the goofing off. All that instead of preparing for what was happening in his life now.

VERDICT

"It's hot," his father said. "I wanted to read the paper outside because your stepmother likes to talk, you know that, so I come out here sometimes because it's quiet. There was a revolution in Nicaragua yesterday, did you hear about it? Just like the one in Cuba. The markets are off because of it. I don't know how much you follow the news."

"I heard about it. I saw something on TV."

"It's good to enjoy yourself. To go out to dinner, see a game. I always encouraged you to have a good time, to have friends. I wanted you to have a good life, I've always wanted that more than anything else. But I can't keep taking care of you like this. You're too old for it."

"Dad."

"I can give you eight hundred a month, that's what I can do. I can't give you fifteen hundred. I don't have it."

"But I need it."

"I know you need it. I know that, Buddy."

HOME

The valet watched while Booker rolled him under the archway to the opened passenger door of Booker's uncle's car, the big sedan still running, the air-conditioning on high. When the chair came close enough, Buddy leaned his weight toward the opening and Booker wrestled first a leg, then a buttock, then the other leg, then Buddy's trunk onto the seat, Buddy grunting, limp, the slick blazer tangled around his midsection. It was like the thorax of an overturned beetle, he thought, and he was starting to laugh when Booker closed the door. But the look Booker gave him through the window came not just from his eyes but from his whole body, lank beneath an unbuttoned shirt with a broad collar. It was a gaze of wholly uninterested, damp-eyed boredom.

UNVEILING

The last occasion on which any number of the Lansky family gathered together in relative harmony was in 1985, for the unveiling of the gravestone of the first Mrs. Meyer Lansky. Somehow Anne...had survived to the age of seventy-four, alone in her West End Avenue apartment with her fur coats, dead birds, and cockroaches. The furs holed and shabby, her hair straggling and unkempt, Anne Lansky had so lost contact with the world that she would leave the door of her efficiency unlocked, to be raided and vandalized by the drug addicts of the seedy neighborhood in which she spent her declining years.

— **Robert Lacey,** *Little Man: Meyer Lansky and the Gangster Life*

ERETZ YISRAEL

Teddy brought him an early dinner that he ate alone on a card table in his study, the blinds drawn, no light but the light of the TV. His breath was short, and after the visit with Buddy he needed to be alone before bed. Eggs, toast, the baseball game a tiring blur. Buddy with maybe a year with some motion in his fingers. Probably less. It was of course a judgment on himself. There was no other way to see it, even if you didn't believe in those things, even if you weren't a religious person.

I PITY THE POOR IMMIGRANT

In Tel Aviv, on Hanukkah, the children and their parents would parade at night with candles and flashlights, a blueness in the dark. There would be a smell of cooking oil, the frying of jelly-filled doughnuts, *sufganiyot,* people out walking, joking, singing, coarse, without self-consciousness. They were a people with their own food, their own dances, their own music, their own language, a people like any other people, at ease in their home. You didn't realize how deformed you were until you saw all that and failed to become a part of it.

> *Prime Minister*
> *Menachem Begin*
> *Jerusalem, Israel.*

Dear Sir:

I won't go into too many overtures and will state my case as briefly as possible.

Mr. Begin, I have a very keen desire to live in Israel, but unfortunately I am verboten. To begin with, when I spent time in Israel, I fell more in love with the country than I was before. My one wish is to be able to spend the rest of my life — which, I presume, can't be too long, as I am 75 yrs. old. . . .

The carbon copies, the folded correspondence, hopes entertained, poorly articulated, doomed.

. . . how much harm can an elderly, sick man do to Israel. . . . I can enter, as I have, any other country without criticism, except the place of my heritage. . . .

If they could see him in the apartment in Miami Beach — Teddy's bed, his bed, the matching nightstands, the wax fruit, the kitchenette. A building of old Jews, waiting with the blinds drawn. After two months of silence, the ministry had responded with another form letter telling him no. He understood by then how much they needed him to be their monster, how secure it made them feel in their righteousness.

I can give you eight hundred a month, that's what I can do.

ANNE

She came to him in a dream as he was sleeping. She perched on his bed and reached down and felt the side of his hip, the angle of the bone, the lip of fat where his waist met his belly. He knew who it was from the smell of her hair, rich with oil, an almost burnt smell. She lay on top of him in her homemade dress, lips pressed shut, breath coming in stabs through her nose.

ANCIENT OF DAYS

The first pass was with torches, the light rising purplish over the red clay ground, cook fires smoldering from the night before. The Israelites came on stolen horses, riding low and at a rearward slouch, braying and screaming, coming out of the hills with the flames in their widespread hands. The Philistine camp was tents and houses more like stables, made of stone and mud, crooked tree limbs holding up the thatched roofs. They used dry thatch screens to block the desert sunlight, and all you had to do was brush them once and the structure collapsed in flames.

The shrieking of women, children, goats, mules. The Philistines begging on their knees. The boys rode through them, trampling and then encircling the ruins so no one escaped. Some dismounted their horses and set about hacking at the villagers with their swords. Those still mounted rounded them up and then the boys on foot slashed backhanded, like harvesters, while the horses reared before them. The farm animals brayed behind the wattle and sticks of their corral. The sun burned more brightly. You could see the pale yellow grass growing up over the red clay. One of the boys could not stop hacking at the head of a corpse, the cheekbone shattered, dark blood running from the nose and eyes. He attacked it with a personal rage until someone finally pulled him away.

PSALM

David saw the green hillside, the distant sheep, the clouds low in the sky casting their giant, slow-moving shadows.

The Lord is my shepherd,
I shall not be in want
He makes me lie down in green pastures,
He leads me beside quiet waters,
He restores my soul.
He guides me in paths of righteousness
For His name's sake.

Even though I walk
Through the valley of the shadow of death
I will fear no evil,
For You are with me;
Your rod and your staff,
They comfort me.
You prepare a table for me
In the presence of my enemies.
You anoint my head with oil;
My cup overflows.
Surely goodness and love will follow me
All the days of my life,
And I will dwell in the house of the Lord
Forever.

WISDOM

It's 2005 — a temporary cease-fire — the Intifada going into its fifth year. We meet at my ex-wife's house in Jerusalem, lantana growing around the iron gates that lead inside. There is chicken *shawarma*, my son Eliav's childhood favorite, but he doesn't eat much. He's clean and cleanly shaven, and dressed in new jeans and a T-shirt and a gray linen sport coat that is unstructured, as if made of paper. His close-cropped hair gives him a look of intelligent severity. He says it's over for real this time, though as we know now it never really ends. Hamas will launch rockets out of Gaza. Soon, there will be another suicide bomber in Netanya. Hezbollah, Hamas, Islamic Jihad, the al-Aqsa Martyrs Brigades. We already know the cease-fire will not last long.

My son's treatment has persuaded him that his addiction has no meaning. It makes no sense to look for causes — to look for causes is to overlook the real cause, which is the addiction itself, and this is to invite relapse. "Don't look for some romance," he tells me. He means don't look for a story, a narrative, a sense of coherence. If this view is what's helpful to him, then it's unhelpful for me to keep probing for more. Even to blame myself, according to this logic, is simply egotistical. But this outlook, so useful in terms of my son's health, is perversely a reinforcement of what for so long has seemed his essential emptiness. When I touch him, he doesn't shrink away or flinch and sometimes he even hugs me back, but he does it consciously — conscientiously — without feeling.

INTERVENTION

By this time, the greater problem was Buddy Lansky's paralysis, which had grown almost total. Buddy had to be fed by someone else, like a baby, and his father found this embarrassing. When there were family gatherings — Meyer's own July Fourth birthday, Buddy's fiftieth birthday in 1980, or a rare visit from Paul — Meyer told his crippled son to arrive early so the feeding could be dealt with before the other guests arrived....

In an attempt to correct his physical decline, Buddy underwent an operation in the early 1980s to realign his neck and the top of his spinal cord. A metal ring was fixed, halolike, around his skull, and the halo was then attached to a back brace, temporarily immobilizing his head. The halo itself was secured to Buddy's skull by metal screws that were wound tightly into the flesh. When Meyer went to visit his son in the hospital, he just could not look at the device.

— **Robert Lacey,** *Little Man: Meyer Lansky and the Gangster Life*

HALO

In the Bible, Absalom — more "highly praised for beauty" than any man in Israel — rises up against his father, David, who has grown decadent and corrupt. Absalom acquires a chariot with horses and fifty men to go running before him. His luxuriant hair, which he cuts only once a year, weighs "twenty shekels by the royal weight." He positions himself as a sympathetic alternative to the king, a man of fairness and integrity, but he is also self-righteous and scheming, a demagogue who steals "the hearts of Israel." Twenty thousand of his charmed followers die in the battle he wages against his father in the forest of Ephraim. As he flees David's troops, Absalom's mule passes beneath a terebinth tree, and his hair catches in the branches and "he dangled between heaven and earth while the mule which was beneath him passed on." He hangs suspended there in agony from this halo, until David's general, Joab, "took three sticks in his palm and he thrust them into Absalom's heart."

Isaac Babel writes, *Stop brawling at your writing-desk and stuttering in the presence of others. Imagine for a moment that you do your brawling on the squares and your stuttering on paper. You are a tiger, you are a lion, you are a cat. You can spend the night with a Russian woman, and the Russian woman will be satisfied with you. You are twenty-five years old. If heaven and earth had rings attached to them, you would seize hold of those rings and pull heaven down to earth.*

David calls to his son Absalom, *My son! My son! Would that I had died in your stead!*

Part Four

Facts on the Ground

12

Ghosts

New York–Jerusalem–Tel Aviv, 2011–12

I have here the first letter Gila sent me back in 2010, before we met that one afternoon for lunch. The letter is still in its envelope, pressed between the pages of a book on Jewish mysticism by the rabbi Adin Steinsaltz. Steinsaltz writes:

> *For everything man does has significance. An evil act will generally cause some disruption or negative reaction in the vast system of the Sefirot; and a good act, correct or raise things to a higher level. Each of the reactions extends out into all of the worlds and comes back into our own, back upon ourselves, in one form or another.*

I look back now over some of the sentences I wrote in 2009 in my piece about David Bellen's murder, thinking of what Steinsaltz says about "reactions":

I had never cared much about Israel — my lack of interest was so long-standing that perhaps I should have wondered more about it. On a deeper level, I might have realized, I had never wanted to face too directly the idea of myself as a Jew.

Perhaps the reason I have never wanted to face too directly the idea of myself as a Jew is that all roads seem to lead to the Holocaust memorial, as if it is the Holocaust that makes one a Jew.

I wrote these sentences almost unthinkingly, as much for the way they sounded as for what they meant. It is in this way that we end up in places we hadn't meant to, the act of the sentences ramifying out and coming back to confront us, "in one form or another," as Steinsaltz puts it, in my case in the form of Gila's first letter. Out of that letter came our meeting. Out of that meeting came this book. *This will interest you,* Bellen's editor, Galit Levy, had written me in her brief note accompanying his long, unpublished essay, "I Pity the Poor Immigrant." *Hope you are well.* When I read "I Pity the Poor Immigrant" for the first time, it reminded me of what Gila had described to me during our lunch with the word *yored,* "the sense of going down, of descending, of being corrupt." I recognized this feeling in Bellen's essay and I recognized it in myself. *Hope you are well.*

We would both always be yordim, Gila had told me, *never* olim. *That was one of the things we had in common.*

What she and Lansky had in common.

What she and I had in common.

In writing this book, I have come to feel like a kind of immigrant in my own life, inhabiting a world of reflections and images of people I can't fully know, some of whom are dead, and I see now that my life has been shaped by this network, in ways I didn't always perceive.

I PITY THE POOR IMMIGRANT

My father was the subject of, and not just a secondary figure in, a newspaper article in the summer of 2011:

> *Lawrence Groff, 76, brother of well-known jewelers Jacob and Beryl Groff, was indicted in federal court yesterday on three counts of conspiracy to commit fraud for his role in an antiques scam that prosecutors say involved a chain of dealers in Britain and Switzerland. The indictment is the latest development in a scandal that has shaken confidence throughout the antiques world, which had already been hard hit by the economic downturn of recent years.*
>
> *According to prosecutors, Groff partnered with London dealer Dennis Lynne, a leading figure in the global antiques market, to sell items of purportedly eighteenth-century English furniture valued at $3 million to buyers in New York and elsewhere. The furniture, according to documents and photographs issued to the court by Lynne's restorer, Martin Briggs, was in fact fabricated by Briggs himself in his Croyden workshop. Briggs claims he made the furniture out of old wardrobes and other items, which he then painstakingly refinished and appointed to look like rare and valuable antiques. In the court documents, Briggs includes invoices submitted to Lynne for about £100,000 (Briggs also asserts that he was never paid for his work). Months later, he learned that Lynne had sold the allegedly eighteenth-century furniture to a dealer in Switzerland for more than ten times that amount. Groff has been charged with arranging for the sale of these forgeries to long-time clients of his in New York and other parts of the U.S.*
>
> *"This is a business based almost entirely on trust," said Candace Ross, an interior decorator in Darien, Connecticut.*

"Trust in a dealer's integrity, his eye, his taste. So not only are we talking about a specific case here, we're talking about the reputation of the antiques market in general."

Ross points out that it can be extremely difficult to ascertain the true value of an antique. Unlike works of fine art, for example, furniture does not usually accrue a paper trail of ownership, or a provenance. A skillful restorer can embellish a legitimately old piece, making it appear rarer and more valuable than it is. A shrewd dealer can then make exaggerated claims about a piece's historical significance.

"It's not so much that Lawrence Groff didn't know what he was doing," said Christian Nabel, a curator at the Metropolitan Museum of Art. "It's more that nobody in that business knows exactly what he's doing. More precisely, people in that business don't want to know exactly what they're doing."

Groff was released on a $200,000 bond. If convicted, he faces up to ten years in prison.

"I knew he was in financial trouble," a friend of Groff's said, "but I didn't know it was serious. If the allegations turn out to be true, and I don't know if they will, then the story will be one about panic, I think. Panic about protecting the kind of life he had built up over many years and was afraid of losing.

"What is the line from Eliot?" the friend continued. " 'The awful daring of a moment's surrender which an age of prudence can never retract'?"

I went to see a friend of mine, Ellen Teague, a few days after this story ran. *I don't have a lot of people in my life,* Gila had told me that day we'd met for lunch. It occurred to me that I didn't have a lot of people in my life either, at least not people I could speak to about my father. Ellen and I have known each other more than twenty years — through her marriage, the birth of her daughter, her divorce, her various boyfriends. During all that time I've been trying to reconcile the way Ellen looks and thinks and speaks with the diminished way she seems to perceive herself. She's a tall woman with a perfect face that she doesn't experience as quite her own, as if the face is a mask. We sat in her office in Carroll Gardens, a room she shares with three other therapists, and drank wine in the late afternoon, chilled white wine on a hot day with the blinds half opened, the still light on the ficus tree and the lime-green sofa and chairs. My father had stopped talking to me a few weeks before this. I told Ellen that although I wasn't surprised by my father's silence, the reality of it now was more powerful than I'd expected. It felt like a verdict. What I meant by that was that it was as if my father was declaring that whatever in our relationship hadn't been my fault before had now become entirely my fault. I felt this, even if I disputed its fairness. I had always been more accusatory than forgiving — I couldn't blame him for this failing of mine. I understood that, even if I saw his silence as most likely a tacit admission of his own guilt, a product of his shame.

"He's not talking to anyone," Ellen reminded me. "It's not just you."

"He's talking to my stepmother."

"They live together. She's his wife."

"She's the one who picks up the phone when I call. She tells me I shouldn't take it personally. Just like you. That I should be patient. That it's not a statement about me. But it certainly is a statement about me."

I realized that the more I talked, the less attached I felt to the words. All I felt was a vague airlessness, which itself was like a product of the room, its smell of carpet cleaner and the gray light leaking in through the blinds. I thought of Ellen's patients, the stories she'd told me about them. They were all from my kind of background, I realized, girls from affluent families who'd experienced some emotional trauma or who'd simply experienced their affluent backgrounds as a kind of emotional trauma. They played out this trauma through the most direct means available to them, anorexia and bulimia, narrowing their days to a simple monotonous punishment of hunger and denial. Food, shit, vomit, blood — all of life's other complexities fell away. Since Ellen herself has struggled with some of these same problems, her work has sometimes seemed to me to have a self-lacerating aspect to it, a dangerous aspect. She lives inside her emotions more than I do. I wouldn't want to have Ellen's emotional life, but I sometimes fear that I've gone too far in the other direction. I do my work because I find it interesting. I cook because I like to eat well. I clean my apartment, I exercise, I see friends, I have occasional men in my life. I have worked all this out to minimize turbulence, but I realize this is ultimately a defensive posture. A part of me thinks that life is meant to be sloppier.

"You haven't told me all that much," Ellen said.

"I don't have anything else to say."

"That can't be true."

"It feels true."

"Then you might want to think about why that is. Just saying."

"Is that your professional opinion?"

"There are art supplies in the closet over there. For the people who don't like to talk or don't know how to talk. The ones who can only draw pictures. Paint. Make things out of clay. I bet you couldn't draw a picture in front of me if I held a gun to your head."

"What is this?"

"I'm just saying it would make sense if you needed some help right now."

"I don't think I need 'help.'"

"Of course not. Everyone thinks that. My clients, for example. Of course eventually there's not really any 'them' to talk to anymore. They're just bodies. Emaciated bodies. That's how committed they are to not talking."

What if everything you have to say is a cliché? Does it change the cliché to express it in other, more evocative language? Or does it make more sense to seek out experiences that don't lead one to feel like a cliché?

"I don't think I'm like your patients," I said to Ellen.

"You mean you're not a lot like them."

"I mean I'm more like the opposite of them."

"Maybe. Maybe so."

But she was right about one thing. It was true that I could hardly imagine anything that would have made me more uncomfortable than opening a pad of fancy drawing paper and trying to sketch out something about my feelings for my father in that office. I wouldn't have known where to begin. If that doesn't make me ridiculous, then I don't know what does.

I was planning to go back to Israel that fall. I wanted to try to find the apartment Gila had shown me in her photographs at lunch. I wanted to talk to David Bellen's ex-wife, the one mentioned in his essay, a woman now named Rachel Kessler. I wanted to talk to Eliav, if he would still talk to me after what I'd written about him in my piece on his father's murder. I wanted to see if I could make

sense of all these disparate lives — certainly I wanted to stop thinking about my own. But it was hard to see it as a story. The story was
too tangled, even as I felt myself getting more and more invested
in it. If I went to Israel, I thought, it would be to simply satisfy a
few of my own curiosities — there was no subject I could claim to
be "investigating" for any possible piece. But then in November I
got an e-mail from Oded Voss, whom I had not heard from in
more than two years. He wrote to tell me that a week before, Eliav
had been found dead of a heroin overdose in Tel Aviv. He was
thirty-eight years old.

———

From an e-mail dated 12/22/2008, forwarded to me from David
Bellen's "Drafts" folder by his ex-wife, Rachel Kessler, on 12/2/2011,
about three weeks before I was to interview her in Jerusalem. The
e-mail was originally addressed to Bellen's friend Adam Harris, an
editor at an American magazine who had rejected Bellen's essay "I
Pity the Poor Immigrant":

> Dear Adam,
>
> I understand your reluctance — the piece is far too
> long — but I wanted to thank you for your kind
> words anyway. What I did not include in the piece was
> yet a further confession. In the fall of 1972, I saw Lan-
> sky once in person. I had been sent to cover his trial,
> not even for a newspaper but for a small journal of lit-
> erature and politics that ceased to exist before it
> could even run my story. My then-wife Rachel and I
> were living in a small one-bedroom flat in Tel Aviv,
> expecting our son Eliav, and we were gravely in need

of money. I took the bus to Jerusalem with no set idea of what I wanted to ask Lansky if I even had the chance.

It turned out of course that he was thronged. It was the day the supreme court handed down its decision denying him citizenship, and afterward I could only see him from a distance, speaking to some newsmen, looking down briefly at the lapel of his suit jacket. I remember that his clothes could not have been more impeccably clean. They shone against his matte skin, making him seem somehow less visible by comparison. I remember his words that day were oddly poetic. He compared his loss to the recent shock of the murder of eleven Israeli athletes at the Olympic Games in Germany. "Look what happened last week in Munich," he said. "Young branches cut down. I'm an old man."

When I returned to our apartment in Tel Aviv that night, it was later than I'd planned and Rachel, pregnant and uncomfortable, was standing in her nightgown at the stove. I had spent the last few hours in the bar at the Dan Hotel, the hotel where Lansky had lived throughout much of his stay in Tel Aviv. It was a place I'd never liked, a place not for Israelis so much as foreigners, yet in my role as "journalist" I somehow felt the need to assert my right to sit there. I hadn't counted on the impact of Lansky's fame, its strange mutedness — I remembered looking at him and marveling and also wondering why I was marveling. I noticed that the sound of his voice, his physical proximity, had caused something profoundly untrustworthy to stir inside me. It was his very mildness that caused this.

At the hotel, a waitress about my own age brought me coffee. When I remained there after the other customers had left, she came for the empty carafe and we ended up talking. She told me she was hoping some day to move to New York. I remember that — at the time, the very words "New York" suggested a place scarcely less romantic and unreal than the one conjured by the matchbooks from Billy Wilkerson's Flamingo Club. I didn't believe she'd ever see New York. I didn't even believe I would. I didn't have any money to take her somewhere when her shift ended — I thought the whole thing was over when I paid my bill. Young, stupid, "poetic" — I can look for words to explain what happened next, but explanations are beside the point. "Impatient" might be the right word. Preyed on by an impatience that made every appetite a panic, something crucial I feared missing out on.

It was about nine months later, a few months after Eliav's birth, that the waitress took me to an apartment in a part of the city that I seldom went to. We walked there all the way from the Dan Hotel. She led me into the foyer of a small gray building and we took the tiny elevator up to the third floor — no one around, no sounds of life, the apartment whose door she opened completely empty — no furniture, not even a single chair, just the bare, scuffed floors. I didn't want to ask for explanations. I guessed that whatever explanation she might have given me would not have been the truth. She ran some water from the tap until it finally ran clear, then she filled a glass that had been left on the counter. The glass could have sat there for years. I watched her slender back beneath her blue dress as she drank. It would have been a few months before the Yom Kippur War, a war which had yet to start but that everybody knew was coming. Almost as much as I remember her, I remember the odd, spartan asylum of that empty apartment, the way we spread our coats like blankets on the floor and laughed a little as we knelt, kissing, then stopped laughing.

The apartment was on Be'eri Street, I remember. More precisely, it was at 4 Be'eri Street, the address my research now tells me was where Meyer Lansky had lived when he wasn't living at the Dan. I've been back to look at the building a few times — I went just yesterday to look at it again. Of course I hadn't seen the apartment yet when I came home that night from Jerusalem, having watched Lansky from afar as he stood outside the Palace of Justice. I closed the door behind me and stood inside the hall and called out Rachel's name, but she didn't answer. I sensed even then that there was a reason she wasn't answering. It was almost midnight and she stood there at the stove with her back to me, wearing her old shapeless robe. She would have been six months pregnant with Eliav. When she finally turned, I had an unmistakable glimpse of my own irrelevance.

Yours,
David Bellen

It was in the business center of a Hampton Inn in Charlotte, North Carolina, that I first read this e-mail. I sat there piecing together its significance beneath the fluorescent light, wondering what I was going to say in three weeks to Bellen's ex-wife, Rachel Kessler, in Jerusalem. Of course Bellen never mentions the waitress's name in his e-mail. I supposed it was possible that she wasn't Gila. I supposed it was possible that there was another waitress at the Dan Hotel who also happened to have an empty apartment in Tel Aviv, or, more plausibly perhaps, that the waitress, whoever it was, had borrowed the apartment from someone else. Perhaps it was at someone else's apartment, and not the one in Gila's photographs, that the waitress had slept with David Bellen in 1973. But perhaps not.

He would have been still in his twenties, Gila, a little older, thirty-four. He comes into the hotel bar and orders coffee, and when he introduces himself the name David Bellen means nothing to her, nothing to anyone at that point. He tells her where he's been — he's been covering the Lansky trial — and she's silent for a moment, but not long enough for him to notice. Everyone in Israel has been following the case. She doesn't react to the name with interest or humor or excitement. Perhaps the young journalist doesn't even tell her his full name. Perhaps he's just David, like so many other Israeli men.

I've been back to look at the building a few times — I went just yesterday to look at it again.

I read that sentence a few times before I referred back to the date of the e-mail's composition. "Yesterday," I realized, was only two days before Bellen had died.

I flew to Ben-Gurion International Airport for the second time in December of 2011, about seven weeks after Eliav's death. I had saved to my cell phone the photograph Gila had taken of us together after our lunch the previous year in New York, that uncomfortable picture in which I seemed to be willing myself into invisibility or ghostliness. "*Strange*," Gila had said that afternoon. *Everyone says that word, "strange."* Of course the photograph I really wished I had on that second trip to Israel was one of the 5×7 prints Gila had shown me of the empty apartment, the apartment I now suspected was at 4 Be'eri Street. I had called Gila's friend Hugh to see if by any chance he'd found those prints among Gila's belongings. I hadn't known until then how naïve a question that was. There are of course services that handle such things, professionals who clean out the houses of deceased people who leave behind no relatives or friends, or whose friends are too busy to sort through the remnants themselves. The 5×7 prints, like so much else that Gila had left behind, had been thrown away.

———

Rachel Kessler was more imposing than I expected — brown, almond-shaped eyes, short dark hair that spoke not just of practicality but of something more like renunciation. She'd been a dancer in her youth and had by all accounts been very beautiful, and you could still see this in the straight, somewhat clerical way she stood, the simple ease of her long oatmeal-colored sweater and her black soft-sided boots. It was the way my mother might have dressed if she were still alive, the way some women artists dress who are Rachel's age. I knew by now that Rachel had grown up not in Israel but in Silver Spring, Maryland, that she had fallen in love with Israel and the idea of Israel on a college semester abroad in 1968. She was twenty-four when she married Bellen, twenty-five when they had Eliav, Rachel still a newcomer, an idealistic young woman who'd left behind a family and a stable life in the U.S. for an unfamiliar country in a state of permanent war. You can take an English-language tour now with Rachel Kessler through the various neighborhoods of Jerusalem, as well as tours of Masada, the Knesset, the Israel Museum, Yad Vashem. On my second day there, I went with her on a tour of Center City, including her own neighborhood, Talbiyeh, where she explained to her group that the Palestinian mansion we saw before us had been abandoned by its original owner only to fall into the care of a Jewish refugee, who'd painstakingly catalogued and stored the house's contents in preparation for the owner's return, though that owner had never returned, and so what could be done? I have seen the contents of such mansions for sale in the flea markets of Tel Aviv — even now you can buy the furniture and china and jewelry of Palestinians who fled in 1948 — but I found myself unable to say anything contradictory to Rachel in front of that audience, unable because of the losses she herself has endured. *It's an interesting story,* she'd said when I'd told her the long, complicated tale of Gila and me. *Nowadays someone like Gila would be a businessperson. She'd be middle class. Maybe a real estate broker. That's where the money is now, of course.* She'd said this and I'd felt that my story, compared to the story of her and Bellen and Eliav, could only make her feel that I wasn't a serious writer, that I was something else, perhaps something more like a member of the paparazzi.

On the afternoon after I followed her tour, we sat at a restaurant near my hotel and talked about Gila, Bellen, Eliav, Lansky, the odd connections between their disparate stories. We had discussed via e-mail the Hebrew word Gila had introduced me to, *yored,* its sense "of going down, of descending, of being corrupt." I reminded Rachel now of the epigraph to Bellen's essay "I Pity the Poor Immigrant," in which the scholar Alan Fried writes of seeing the world through "the gangster's eye," the eye that views the world as divided into contrary groups of "wolves and lambs, predators and victims, winners and losers, deceivers and deceived." I gathered that Bellen saw himself and Eliav through that lens while writing the piece and I wondered what Rachel thought about this.

"I'm sorry to keep reminding you of such unpleasant things," I said when she didn't answer at first.

She looked at her fingers on the stem of her glass of wine. "It's not all unpleasant," she said. "They were people I loved. Both of them, very much. In any case, you don't have to remind me of those unpleasant things. They're always there."

What made it difficult to talk about all this, she told me, was what she could only describe as an uncanny element to the rift between Bellen and Eliav. They'd been at odds from the very beginning, she told me, the rift so fundamental that it seemed predetermined, genetic. Eliav was quiet, inward, watchful. Bellen was not exactly loud but he could be exuberant, even when he didn't want to be. It was a side of himself he sometimes struggled to suppress in his writing, his South Tel Aviv boisterousness, his coarseness, and this, Rachel thought, was the basis of the problem between him and Eliav, even from the very beginning. Before Eliav could possibly understand any of this, he picked up on his father's mild shame, intuited it somehow in his father's posture, his occasional evasiveness or furtiveness. Bellen's exuberance, which was much stronger than this shame, perversely made Eliav even more silent, more watchful — his father's irreverence and gaiety seemed to embarrass or disappoint Eliav, who became quieter as he grew more aware of his own scorn.

"He was ten when David left," Rachel went on. "But of course he knew it was coming — we both knew that. David couldn't help himself, it was the way he was made. There were a lot of women. I didn't like it, I was furious with him, but I loved him. I couldn't help but love him. But Eliav was always there too, in the background, and he would have to witness the tension between us, no matter how much we tried to conceal it from him. It made David begin to move farther and farther away, not only because of me and my anger but because Eliav was always there, watching it all."

It was a warm enough afternoon even in December that we were sitting on the porch beside a wall of gold-colored Jerusalem stone, surrounded by succulent plants and cacti, protected from the sun's glare by white panels slung like sails from black cords above our heads. When the waitress brought our food, she wore a starched apron and a man's dark necktie. It was not unlike the restaurant at which Gila and I had had lunch in New York the previous year, I told Rachel. The menu's graphics were like something from New York — like something from anywhere, I realized. Roasted eggplant with sriracha remoulade, summer rolls with duck breast and avocado, endive salad with Sainte-Maure cheese. All over the world now, everywhere you go, there's a restaurant that will know how to make the most of whatever is charming about its faded neighborhood and will present it in some understated, idiosyncratic way.

"The affairs made him paranoid and extreme," Rachel said, speaking again of Bellen. "In his personal life, of course, but also in the way he saw the whole world. Because the world is also like this: a glass of white wine on a nice day. Even in Israel, it's like this. I don't think he ever really accepted that. In his imagination there was never any room for forgiveness, no room for healing. It bored him, my forgiveness. It was worse than that — it disgusted him. So eventually I had to stop trying to forgive him."

I thought of the Ivan Schwebel painting that Bellen refers to in his Lansky essay, the image of King David's first wife, Michal, confronting him on the street at night as in a Hollywood movie, "her eyes moist and accusing in the way of a betrayed woman." *He has indeed betrayed her and he will betray her further and in the picture both he and his first wife seem to already know this,* Bellen wrote. I'm not comfortable when people cry, particularly people I don't know, in a public place in a foreign country. I guess no one is comfortable with it. *Touch her hand,* I told myself. *Say you're sorry.* I did these things, and Rachel smirked as she kept sniffling, ashamed of herself.

"Eliav hardly inherited anything from David," she said then. "But I think it upset him to take what little there was. It will sound simplistic, but I think taking that money was what led to his relapse, his overdose. It took a long time, almost three years, but I think that was the root of it."

For everything man does has significance. An evil act will generally cause some disruption or negative reaction in the vast system of the Sefirot; and a good act, correct or raise things to a higher level. Each of the reactions extends out into all of the worlds and comes back into our own, back upon ourselves, in one form or another.

I thought, *wolves and lambs, predators and victims, winners and losers, deceivers and deceived.* Except of course that everyone is all of those things. God says to David, *And so now, the sword shall not swerve from your house evermore.* The sword that comes from outside, in the form of enemies, but also the sword that comes from inside, the sword with which we bifurcate ourselves.

In this way, everyone is *yored* in the end.

At her house back in Talbiyeh, Rachel showed me some of Eliav's belongings, which she had in boxes and flat files in her study. In particular, she showed me an oil painting made by Eliav when he was only seventeen, a portrait of his father, Bellen. The poet's homely face was depicted as it was — craggy, eccentric, bespectacled — but with a willful ugliness that rendered it some-how beautiful. The cheekbones and the eye sockets were etched in thick jagged lines, blacks and reds and beiges, like some mask from a thousand years ago. It seemed to have been painted, like all the other work of Eliav's that Rachel showed me that afternoon, out of a pure and purely unreflective talent. Eliav had been a prodigy, it turned out. That both the artist and his subject were dead now gave the painting of his father an uncanny sense of per-manence. There was the watcher and the watched, forever fixed in that relationship.

There were sketchbooks from his high school years, along with photo albums of more elaborate pieces — paintings and also sculp-tures of clay, papier-mâché, and even cast bronze. It's the sketch-books, though, that I remember particularly well. In them, Eliav would spend five or six consecutive pages executing colored draw-ings in the styles of various modern masters: Cézanne, Picasso, Matisse, Klee, Kandinsky, Pollock, De Kooning. Five or six pages would be all it took for him not only to master the particular vocab-ulary of the artist he was imitating but to ingeniously explore it in different ways through his own inventions. There were no blank pages, no false starts or scratch-outs, no sheets removed. The sketch-book was like a primer on twentieth-century art, executed by a highly skilled draftsman who if anything was a little too skilled. The talent was a kind of shorthand, all technique. I wondered what someone would do with that kind of talent once they got old enough to learn that it was not the same as making "art," that in fact "art" as it exists now has practically nothing to do with such technique.

There was another artifact from Eliav's youth that I remem-ber, though it was not impressive in the same way — it was, per-haps deliberately, unimpressive on the level of technique. It was a series of black-and-white photographs that Eliav had taken in the streets of Tel Aviv in the late 1980s and early '90s — portraits of ordinary people, working people, men and women in dry cleaners, supermarkets, hair salons, bakeries, garages. The subjects were never looking into the camera. Instead the images had a random, even accidental quality — a quality of neutral surveillance, of ordinary people not realizing they were being looked at — that made them more haunting. I think Eliav understood that these photographs were haunting and perhaps he even understood why. I think this because of a quotation he thought to include on the last page of the album in which he'd arranged the photographs at the age of eighteen. The quotation, from Kafka, was in Hebrew, but Rachel paraphrased it for me (I have given it here as translated by Willa and Edwin Muir):

In a light that is fierce and strong one can see the world dissolve. To weak eyes it becomes solid, to weaker eyes it shows fists, before still weaker eyes it feels ashamed and smites down him who dares to look at it.

Rachel's husband, Dov, had come quietly into the study and stood behind her now where she was seated in her chair, his hand on her shoulder. He was gruff, nearly silent, a white-haired and white-bearded physicist in an expensive blue suit and yarmulke.

"We've been going through these old boxes," Rachel said to me then. "It was such a strange thing — we just happened to be moving to this new house right when Eliav died. I guess in some ways that was good. It obviously gave us something else we had to think about."

She had the album of photographs still in her lap. There was another thing she wanted to tell me that afternoon, it turned out, something she'd never told anyone before, except for Dov. She told me that Eliav used to say that he had a recurring nightmare. In this recurring nightmare, he was forced to stand in an empty room and watch while his father was executed.

"I always thought that was strange," she said, looking down, the photo album in her lap now forgotten, unseen. "Not for the obvious reason, but because I had never thought of it as happening in a room. I had pictured it happening outside. But in the nightmare it would happen in a room. An empty room. 'I was in the room where it happened,' Eliav would say."

———

In my hotel room that night, I read *Haaretz*, then the *Jerusalem Post*, all the while the TV news on in the background, a stream of images accompanied by words I couldn't understand. Apart from Iran and the fear of Iran, the news seemed to be largely about fanaticism — extremist Jewish settlers who had attacked an Israeli military base in the West Bank, some ultra-Orthodox men who had spat on a young girl walking to school in clothes they deemed insufficiently modest. Though I'd arrived just a few days ago, Israel was already unlike what I remembered from my last trip. I felt surrounded this time not by ancient intractable conflict but by cynical gloating — Orthodox women in clothes so unflattering you wondered where they found the stores that sold such items, their sons in football jerseys and basketball shoes and embroidered *kippot*. I connected my laptop to the hotel's Wi-Fi and looked further into the story about the settlers who'd attacked the military base. John Walker Lindh — that's who they reminded me of — the suburban American boy who through aimless disaffection had wound up joining the Taliban. The settlers, I learned, were part of a broader movement known as the Hilltop Youth, who desecrated mosques,

assaulted Palestinians and destroyed their fields, and had now
attacked one of Israel's own military bases. It was a photograph, as
it often is, that sealed my interest. The image seemed to encapsu-
late all the contradictions of this group of mostly young men and
their romanticized relationship to violence — the organic farming
in the desert, the camping and mountaineering T-shirts, the scraggly beards and *talisim* and ornate skullcaps, their remote outposts
consisting of corrugated aluminum sheds, or just tents and old
sofas, plastic tarps and rifles and guitars. The incoherent need to
believe in something — the need that then goes looking for a
cause, an ideal. Fighting the Man. Fighting the Palestinians.
Fighting nothing. I had a sudden waking dream there in my hotel
room of David Bellen being marched across a field by some of
those boys in their beards and cargo pants. I saw it very clearly: Bellen struggling forward over the rocky ground, stooped over and
handcuffed, his arms exposed by the short sleeves of a stained
white undershirt. His glasses were broken, his face smeared with
blood. He was like an animal left in their care, a repository of some
collective shame that had to do with the boys' need to punish him.
Whatever game they were playing now was played solemnly, without words, without taunting or joy. It was obvious that Bellen knew
what would happen next.

———

The place I walked to the next morning was Me'a Shearim, the
center of ultra-Orthodox Jerusalem, once a planned neighborhood of garden apartments for middle-class secular Jews, now
a slum without gardens, trees, or vegetation of any kind.
The cement or concrete buildings had deteriorated into something that looked remarkably like a modern version of an

eighteenth-century shtetl, a place of sagging floors and flaking paint, no ornament other than the practicalities of business signs and political and religious bulletins. Laundry hung in the spaces between the beige and gray buildings. Car exhaust, litter, broken toys. It was a shtetl not by design but by choice, a ghetto or a Lower East Side slum not by design but by choice. If I'd been less irrational that morning, I might have remembered that no one had asked me to go to Me'a Shearim — in fact, there were large signs urging strangers not to intrude. It was the Sabbath, and would be the third night of Hanukkah, and so there were people out shopping for the evening meal, the storefronts open to reveal a few pale apples, onions, sacks of potatoes. I felt like a stranger in the broadest sense. "Strange," because although the people around me were Jews, as was I, none of them looked at me, not even by accident, not once. The men wore black hats and dark suits with white shirts, or they wore outlandish silk robes and silk stockings, round fur-trimmed crowns called *shtreimlech*. The women were sexless, all but invisible. I was from some other place and time — probably I wasn't a Jew at all in their minds. Rachel had invited me to Shabbat dinner at her house that night but I had declined, because in addition to Hanukkah and Shabbat, it was also the third anniversary of David Bellen's murder. I imagined the prayers and rituals I wouldn't know, the *yahrzeit* candle in its glass, and I thought of Gila's word *yored*. The prayers and rituals in light of that word seemed like ash from some fire that had burned through generations of strangers who happened to be my ancestors. I didn't want to speak to my ancestors. I didn't want to hear what they thought of me.

In a light that is fierce and strong one can see the world dissolve. To weak eyes it becomes solid, to weaker eyes it shows fists, before still weaker eyes it feels ashamed and smites down him who dares to look at it.

Dumpsters, air-conditioning units, the street beneath my feet crumbling and rutted with potholes, almost a dirt road in places. I tried to remember that the people before me were meant to be uninterested in the griminess of the physical world, that in their devoutness they were focused instead on the imminent, holy presence beneath its surface. But the more I looked at them, the more I thought of another passage from Kafka:

What have I in common with Jews? I have hardly anything in common with myself and should stand very quietly in a corner, content that I can breathe.

———

The third anniversary of Bellen's murder. When I got back to my hotel that afternoon, I looked over the piece I'd written about it in 2009, particularly at the ending, where I quote an e-mail, presumably from Oded Voss, tying the murder to organized crime:

He arranges a deal—his letters and papers, worth more when he's dead, sold through someone who could get their full worth, someone from his old neighborhood. Proceeds will go to the useless son. The son has no idea about any of this. Any number of scenarios after that. Maybe Bellen's broker/collaborator is so disgusted by the idea of Bellen contemplating all this that he kills Bellen himself, just because he can. Maybe that was somehow implied in their conversation all along. Maybe Bellen killed himself. Maybe they drove him to Beit Sahour and let him blow his own brains out behind a construction site. Maybe they let him do it in Tel Aviv. The people I'm talking about can arrange these things anywhere. They hate the Arabs but they also work with the Arabs. Was it Bellen's inspiration or theirs to dump the body in Beit Sahour?

I realized that after almost three years I no longer believed in these theories of the crime. They spoke to me now more of the theory's probable creator, Oded Voss, than of the mystery itself. I thought of what Rachel had said, that Eliav had inherited only a small amount of money. I thought of Eliav's nightmare. *"I was in the room where it happened," Eliav would say.* I thought of my waking dream the day before of those boys with their rifles marching Bellen across the rocky field.

I went to Tel Aviv that Monday, still not having managed to talk to Voss since my arrival. We'd been playing phone tag, perhaps half deliberately, and so when I got to Tel Aviv I went by myself to Bellen's childhood neighborhood, Hatikvah, and to the steakhouse on Etzel Street that Voss had taken me to the last time we'd been together. I had forgotten how small the restaurant was, how brightly lit. There on the side wall were those signed and framed photographs of Israeli athletes and politicians and movie stars, along with a picture of the former owner, Yehezkel Aslan, one of the gangsters who appears in *Kid Bethlehem*. I chose a table behind the only other customers, a pair of Mizrahi men seated before a spread of a dozen salads in tiny dishes, pita bread, kebabs. One was on his cell phone, the other talked to the waitress while he fingered a large stack of shekel notes beside two other stacks in rubber bands. I realize how unreal that sounds, how like a movie, but it's the paradox of places like the steakhouse that they don't seem quite real, even when you're there. Bellen's picture was not on the wall — it hadn't been there before either, but the absence struck me this time as deliberate, ghostly. Perhaps I was wrong about Voss's theory. Perhaps outside the restaurant, somewhere in Hatikvah, Bellen's killers really were still at large.

I went for a walk after lunch through the outdoor market, a place oddly reminiscent of a large train station, with its rows of prefabricated stalls, roofed by large white plastic panels like the ones at the restaurant at which I'd had lunch with Rachel. People browsed through bins of multicolored candies, dried fruits, nuts, spices, olive oil, the women dragging behind them those graceless wheeled carts made of plaid vinyl, the men carrying their purchases in pale orange plastic bags. Shoes, key chains, wallets, kitchenware, plungers. The drama of buying and selling, a thousand actors playing themselves with a slightly heightened vigor amid the dry goods and the bins laden with produce. Not ghostly Me'a Shearim but strident Tel Aviv. Not the pious in their ghetto but ordinary people focused on the simple comings and goings of daily life. I walked all the way back to my hotel through the parts of the city that Eliav would have known, endless stretches of shabby little shops, noise, buildings the color of wet cement, traffic, smog. In Levinsky Park, crowds of African men loitered or waited for day work, refugees from war and genocide in Eritrea and South Sudan, their belongings in shopping carts or just piled beside a tree — foam pads, carpets, blankets. Homeless people without status in a country frightened by their arrival. Not far from where they gathered was the bus station, where Eliav had bought drugs in his twenties and early thirties and perhaps again that November. It was a few blocks down from the no-man's-land on either side of Highway 20, a place of vacant lots full of dust and weeds and the abandoned shell of what might once have been a municipal garage, now covered in graffiti. The wasteland around that highway reminded me of Bellen's conjuration of Eliav in the midst of one of his relapses. *He remembers something about a sign that says PAZ — blue letters on a yellow ground, PAZ — but what he no longer knows is if this sign was a part of his friend's directions or whether its vivid colors and letters have only made it seem that it was part of those directions.* I took a photograph of the abandoned

garagelike structure — it didn't have a sign that said PAZ but the graffiti on it called out to me for reasons I could only guess at in that moment. I learned later that the graffiti was a religious invocation. It was the name of a revered Hasidic rabbi, Nachman of Breslov, who among other things wrote mystical tales that influenced Kafka.

That afternoon, I went back to my hotel near the beach. I sat at the bar off the sunlit lobby and looked at the picture on my cell phone of Gila and me, more and more perturbed by the expressionless look on my face, the quality of numb detachment, even immateriality. I remembered that lunch we'd had, the sense I'd gotten then that Gila, in her illness and isolation, somehow thought of us as kindred spirits. I felt that kinship myself now, sitting at the hotel bar, imagining Gila as a waitress thirty years ago, keeping her back straight as she bent down with a balanced tray of drinks. I suppose the kinship I really felt was not so much with Gila as with her absence, or with whatever faint traces I imagined still remained of her in Tel Aviv. I had learned from the manager at the Dan Hotel that a Gila Konig had been an employee there from 1969 to 1977. No one who worked there now of course had ever met her. I couldn't find any information about what she'd done between 1977 and 1980, the year she finally came to New York. It occurred to me that I was probably the last person in Israel who still knew her name.

When I finished my drink, I walked up Frishman Street, past Ben Yehuda, Dizengoff, the sudden open spaces of what is now called Rabin Square — pigeons and litter, discount stores fronted by cafés with white tables. I had been walking all day and I kept walking now, into a neighborhood of modern apartment buildings, flowering trees, benches in the shade, the streets named for artists and musicians. At 4 Be'eri Street, I found the building — the ordinary building that Lansky's biographer Robert Lacey describes as a "run-down concrete box on stilts that was similar to thousands of others in the suburbs of Tel Aviv." Through the window of one of the apartments I could see simple birch furniture, a lamp on the ceiling in the reds and blacks of a Calder mobile. There was no one else out on the street and so I came closer, following the sidewalk to a pair of clipped hedges that led to the entryway. Nine buzzers on a metal doorjamb. The kind of building that in my childhood in New York would have contained the office of a podiatrist or an orthodontist. I looked through the glass door and saw the dim foyer with its low ceiling, the beige linoleum on the walls and floor — looking through that glass was like looking at a photograph from 1972, a black-and-white photograph of a crime scene. *Almost as much as I remember her, I remember the odd, spartan asylum of that empty apartment, the way we spread our coats like blankets on the floor and laughed a little as we knelt, kissing, then stopped laughing.*

Bellen had remembered it thirty-five years later, the run-down concrete box on stilts that was similar to thousands of others in the suburbs of Tel Aviv. As for Gila, she had almost certainly forgotten about Bellen by the time she told me her story. It was not Bellen but Lansky she wanted to tell me about, Lansky who made her story matter. I thought about all three of them having entered this nondescript building where I now stood. To stare in through the glass of its door was to understand insignificance not as a desert or a sea or a night sky but as nothing at all, as a silence.

Every once in a while she went back to the apartment to see that it was still there, still waiting for her. Three empty rooms with marks on the bare white walls from where the furniture had stood, where the pictures had hung. Broken slats in the closet door. The water in the kitchen sink would sputter out brown until it ran clear. Such a strange, unwanted gift, as if he were finally telling her something crucial.

I had started writing this book already, before I'd actually seen the building. Standing there outside it, I heard in my head how the first section should end.

The next evening I walked into the lobby of the Dan Hotel to finally meet Voss. I had made a point of arriving late, not wanting to have to sit there waiting for him, not sure I even wanted to see him again, but there he was, sitting in the far corner in one of the gray armchairs in the faint light reading a newspaper. The windows' tinted glass, even with the Mediterranean glare behind it, created a muted stillness, as if time had stopped and no one else would ever enter that room, or try to leave it — dark brown walls, brushed steel tables, black and gray chairs arranged in precise geometrical groups. Voss didn't stand when he saw me coming, even though the room is vast in a way that would have caused most people to stand or at least shift in their seat. He wore a charcoal suit with a white dress shirt that had thin gold panes. He was a little more heavyset than I remembered, or perhaps it was just that his beard had grown in more thickly than before — that beard and the tousled graying hair were so tirelessly deployed, all the more effective for being so. As I walked toward him, he put two fingers to the bone behind his ear and let his elbow rest on the arm of his chair, looking at me, not trying to pretend otherwise.

"I'm sorry about Eliav," he said, after we said hello. "He meant something to you. I should have been more aware of that."

I tilted my head, dismissing what now seemed like a tired sentiment. I'd been angry the last time we'd spoken, over Skype, the little box with Voss's face in it pixelated and badly lit, as if he were sitting in a cell, speaking against his will. If he'd told me about Eliav earlier, I'd insisted, I could have gone to the funeral, but we both knew I wouldn't have flown all that way for the funeral, that

I'd barely known Eliav. I was angry for other reasons. Angry for who knew what reasons.

"He was a little tragic," I said. "But you were right about him. He was poisonous."

"It must be hard having a father like that and not having any talent of your own."

"He did have talent. But he was also poisonous." I put my purse on the glass tabletop and sat down, looking abstractedly for the waiter. "Everyone's family is poisonous. Isn't yours?"

"My parents are Holocaust survivors." He folded his newspaper with a firm crease and left it resting on the table. "Small, gentle people who came through it all and loved everything my brother and I did. That's another kind of problem."

We ordered drinks — a red wine for me, a club soda for Voss. I told him then that I'd read his book when it came out in English last year. It was about his combat duty in the First Lebanon War, a memoir written in the voice of Voss's nineteen-year-old self, a boy sarcastically eager for the very trauma that would soon diminish him. Near the end, Voss accidentally shoots a civilian on the outskirts of Beirut, a sixteen-year-old girl he sees running between two houses. When he comes to clear the area, having panicked and fired on her, he finds that she's not quite dead. A bubble of blood and saliva pulses from her lips, her breathing shallow and rapid, her eyes open but fixed. He is standing right above her where she lies on the ground but he is incapable of putting her suffering to an end. He shoots once at her head and misses to the left, then shoots again and misses to the right. The sounds the girl makes are almost sexual — he recognizes it from the movies, not from experience — little moans each time he fires and misses. I told him now how sad I thought the book was, how sad for all its cynicism.

"I think about you sometimes," he said then.

"I wouldn't have expected you to think about me."

"Why not?"

"I don't know. I guess, what, I'm insecure."

"I'm sorry things worked out the way they did the last time. I read your Bellen piece. There were other things that happened between us too. Better things. You didn't write about those things quite as much."

The drinks came, and then after a silence he finally sighed and said he couldn't stay long, he had work the next day. He looked down at his hand on the table — impatience, contempt, I wasn't sure what he was feeling at that moment. I was surprised by the solemn cast to his face. I saw how easy it would be to touch his hand, to run my fingers down the cuff of his jacket to his wrist — I wanted to touch him and I didn't really understand why. The last time I'd touched him, more than two years ago, he had hit me.

"I sometimes thought about you too," I said then, sipping my wine. "But then I thought about how you live here and I live there and what a waste of time it would be to keep thinking about you."

He reached across the table and put his hand on my bare arm. I thought he might even try to kiss me, but he just looked at his hand there. It was a physical sensation, I told myself, only that. It was mostly just a consequence of doing this story, almost a coincidence in that way.

I told him the story of Gila then, sitting there in the mostly empty lobby of the Dan Hotel, showing him the pictures I'd taken on Be'eri Street, and the picture of Gila and me at lunch. Gila and

Lansky. Gila and Bellen. Gila and my father. I could somehow
sense that Voss didn't believe all or even most of what I was saying,
that he was even more incredulous than I might have expected,
but I could also sense that incredulity for Voss was a common
enough feeling — he'd heard a lot of stories he didn't believe. If he
was surprised to find me purveying another such story, then he
was also forbearing. It was as if he thought it could happen to anyone, not deliberately lying but believing and then recounting a
story that could never be verified.

———————

Later, he parked on the street across from my hotel — I couldn't
afford to stay at the Dan — and we walked past the African guard
into the drab lobby with its glass tables and Judaica. There were
people sleeping on the couches with their luggage, waiting for
check-in time the next morning. It was the last night of Hanukkah
and there were menorahs out with eight candles burning in each,
as well as a large electric menorah with waxy plastic arms, all of
them lit up orange. Something about the plastic menorah made
me wonder if I was going to be able to sustain whatever impulse
had led me this far with Voss. There was a crowd in the elevator,
Orthodox Jews speaking French. They didn't look at us.

My clothes were scattered all over my tiny room. It was a
glimpse into my life, like opening a diary. He reached for me — not
hard but just testing it, touching my arm, above the elbow. He was
a head taller than me, and I had to tilt my face up when he pushed
his fingers into the hair at the base of my skull and leaned over
me. His mouth tasted like cigarettes, but I wanted him and so the
staleness just tasted like Voss, his old indifferent self. The room

was too dark when I switched off the lights, so I left the one on in the bathroom. It cast a faint reflection on the glass of the framed painting opposite the bed. It doesn't happen often, the slide into a vagueness that you didn't instigate or even try to shape. The feeling takes in the shadows of the room, the orange glow behind the window, the clock radio and the phone on the night table. His BlackBerry buzzed from the pocket of his pants on the floor, the ringer turned off. It would buzz for a while, then stop, then buzz once more when someone left a message.

"I didn't expect all this," I said.

His face was just above mine, his lips not far from my ear. "You know my story now. The war story."

"You never thought about living somewhere else after a story like that?"

"That story's the reason I have to live here."

"Then I guess I don't understand."

"I don't expect you to understand. I'm just explaining why."

———

My flight left a little before midnight the next night. Voss put my luggage in the trunk and then he sat in the driver's seat, his face dim in the angled glow of the streetlight, his beard harsh against his cheek. His little black car had a combination lock that made loud shrill beeps when he punched in the code in the dark. I touched the sleeve of his coat and he held my hand for a second or two, then put the car into gear. We drove onto the highway toward the airport, listening to the radio, the commentator reporting the news in Hebrew in a voice somehow urgent but reassuring at the same time. I couldn't understand anything he was saying, but I took in the general ambience. It was as if his reporting of the

events in such a sane tone could render those events harmless,
rational rather than emotional, almost theoretical. I asked Voss
once again about the investigation into Bellen's death and he told
me, as he'd told me many times, that investigations like that seldom yield results, that cases like Bellen's are almost never solved. I
realized that knowing who actually killed Bellen no longer mat-
tered as much to me as it once had. I realized that it would only
lead to the greater mystery of why anyone kills anyone — why violence persists and why we continue believing or hoping that someday it will stop. That was the question Bellen explored in his work,
the reason he wrote *Kid Bethlehem* and the reason he wrote "I Pity
the Poor Immigrant." It was not in the hope of finding an answer,
I thought, but in the hope of creating a space in which to think
through the question. He was thinking about it in the days before
he died, I knew now, walking to the apartment at 4 Be'eri Street
where he and Gila and Lansky had all found a few moments of
respite in a country that, perhaps more than any other, fore-
grounds the transience of our lives.

At the airport, I gave Voss a kiss and looked into his eyes. You
want to close your eyes, but if you leave them open and look it's a
way of holding on to them. There in the drop-off lane I kept my face
close to his for a long moment. The fatigue made everything light,
slow, increasingly deliberate. I was thinking of my father — that old
cliché about the allure of unavailable men. But as that other old cliché goes, clichés are always truer than we'd like to believe. Perhaps
I was just more simplistic than I liked to believe. More simplistic
and more adrift.

"I'll see you," I said.

"I hope so."

"You will. You'll come to New York."

We said goodbye and he watched me as I walked my suitcase

through the terminal's sliding doors and headed for the check-in line. I didn't turn around. I should say that I imagine he was watching me as I walked through the doors.

———

That May, they started jury selection in my father's trial. I thought, *I should call him. He should call me.* But I was in the middle of writing this book and we both knew that in some ways this book, like most of my writing, is a commentary on us, on our past. My father knew that I was including him here not only because of what he has told me but because of what he hasn't told me. Because of what I suspect, not only about his current predicament but about his life. *You're my daughter,* he'd said when I told him I was going ahead with this project. Even then, I don't think it was just the story of his affair with Gila that troubled him. I think it was the larger story and the fact that I was going to place him inside it. I had never thought I had the kind of family it was possible to "dishonor" — my family wasn't given to such old-fashioned notions — but that's one way I found myself interpreting his silence now. The more I thought about it, the more I understood this book as a kind of betrayal. I don't have any children of my own. I have never wanted children and I no longer know what that says about me. I know and have known for a long time now that my alienation is just alienation, not a sign of any deeper spiritual insight. I know that, but I don't know what to do with the alienation itself. There's a condition called Jerusalem Syndrome in which visitors to the city fall into religious-tinged delusions or even psychosis, as if the very atmosphere there is permeated with madness. The affected people tend to recover shortly after they return home. Almost all of them do.

I PITY THE POOR IMMIGRANT

A King David psalm:

. . . I am poured out like water,
And all my bones are out of joint;
My heart is like wax;
It is melted within me.

My strength is dried up like a potsherd;
And my tongue cleaves to my jaws;
And you lay me in the dust of death.

I went to see Gila's friend Hugh that spring. I told him I'd found
the building in Tel Aviv but that I'd never know for sure if Gila's
story was true or not. He showed me some more photographs — Gila at the beach, Gila at her house in Sag Harbor, Gila
at a party for her birthday in a simple black dress and two strands
of pearls. Her smile as she posed between Hugh and his partner,
their heads brought close together to fit in the frame, was more
vivacious than I would have imagined possible. An image began
to emerge of Gila remade as an American, practically assimi-
lated — more or less ordinary, more or less happy. I remembered
something Rachel Kessler had told me in Jerusalem. *Because the*
world is also like this: a glass of white wine on a nice day. Even for
someone like Gila, even for someone like me. As a kind of parting
gift, Hugh gave me something he'd taken as a keepsake from her
house. It was a framed poster from the thirties, a black-and-white
photo of the designer Elsa Schiaparelli, her name at the bottom,
and at the top, in pink letters, the single word *Shocking!*

"Don't take it if you don't want it," he said.

But of course I did take it. Like everything else, I included it in this book. I have it here now in the alcove in my apartment. Procrastinating, checking e-mail, I get a note from Voss that says, *Skype me. Here for another hour.* It's one o'clock in the morning where he is, in his office in Jerusalem. We chat on our respective screens, his facial gestures split up somewhat like the panels in a comic strip, the picture frozen, then in motion again, then frozen. I sometimes wish I didn't write about these subjects. I have told myself many times that I write about violence to understand it, not just out of morbid curiosity, but it can often seem like a fine distinction. It can seem like a distinction without a difference. I tell this to Voss and he says that the world we live in is more perverse than people like to think. He tells me about a recent murder in Ramat Gan in which the killers shot their victim in his own garage. He barked like a dog when they shot him, the killers said, and they were being literal. The victim's wife, who was inside the house, came out to the garage because she'd heard a dog barking and she thought it was strange that there would be a dog in the garage because they didn't own a dog.

"I'm just a journalist," Voss says. "I'm not, what, a belletrist like you."

"I don't know what I am," I say.

"You're a voyeur. Like me. So what? There are worse things."

His face is fixed on the screen again, then the screen goes gray, an entirely textureless blank. His disembodied voice tells me then that he's considering coming to New York in a few months. It's something we've talked about before. When we've talked about it, I've always realized that it would mean him staying for at least a week, probably closer to two. A round-trip ticket between Ben-

Gurion and JFK is about fourteen hundred dollars with tax, a lot of money.

"We hardly know each other," I say, still unable to see him clearly.

"I'd say we know each other in some ways," his voice says.

"In some ways maybe."

"I'm asking if you want me to come or not."

His image reappears, moving once more in that stuttering way. I see his beard, the pupils of his eyes, the ring at the end of the zipper of his sweater. His face pulses in and out of clarity — stark, shadowed, volatile. There seems to be no answer in that moment other than to say yes. I tell him okay. His face is there and then not there, the light shifting as if I'm seeing him through flames.

Part Five

Epilogue

13

The End

One of the boys was tugging on the sleeve of Eliav's jacket now, a different boy this time, his hair grown out in black curls that were almost like stubby dreadlocks. The standing water on the floor rose above the tops of their shoes. In front of them, a rectangle of yellowish light shone weakly on the far wall, cast there by a humming carousel slide projector that sat on a long card table at the room's rear corner. It was dark except for that rectangle of light and the center of the room, where two floodlamps clipped to the ceiling pipes lit up a listless body seated in a chair, the bare bulbs burning a fierce white inside the opened corollas of their housings.

The body in the chair was Eliav's father, Bellen. They had stripped him to his undershirt, his broken glasses strapped around his head with what appeared to be shoelaces. The sides of his father's head were smeared dark with blood. Eliav had heard the screams from outside, a gun at his back, his face against the concrete fence. Seeing his father now, he found it impossible to stop looking. His father sat in the chair beneath the floodlights with an almost childlike inattention, the lenses of his broken glasses glinting in the bright light. They'd given Eliav the pistol by then, a Jericho 941, its dark grip textured in a grid pattern that had no temperature. He felt it in his hand, the smooth-rough surface of the metal. There was a thinness to his breathing, which caught in his throat like a little boy's.

"I don't know what he thought, that we were going to make it easy for him?" said the one in the denim jacket who was standing between Eliav and his father. He sniffed and shook his head, scratching his neck, the torn cuff of the jacket hanging from his forearm. He held a bandanna with which he'd been dabbing his sweat, and he let the rag drop now with a slow splash into the standing water.

"All those ideas of his, that's why you're here now. You're here because he was asking for this — not this exactly, but you know what I mean. He wanted to be some kind of martyr. A martyr for what? Or maybe he just wanted to die. I don't really know."

He turned to Bellen then. "Look who's here," he said. "Does it make it easier to know that he's here? That your son will remember all this, just like in the old prayers?"

His father looked scalded and pale beneath the bright lights, his hair glistening like a baby's hair, his eyebrows almost transparent.

The boy looked back at Eliav then, fierce, his jacket twisted off his shoulder, boots splashing in the water. "Show some mercy, you piece of shit," he said. "Don't you think he's a little ready for it to be over with?"

The water smelled like dead fish and gasoline. It was cold on Eliav's feet, saturating his shoes. His father raised his chin just enough for the lenses of his glasses to stop reflecting the light of the floodlamps. It was impossible to see any movement or color in those eyes.

He felt the way his hand conformed to the pistol's grip, the easy way his fingers fit around its contours. He felt the heft of the gun and the tension behind the trigger and the pressure of the metal against his skin. The boy in the denim jacket was still talking. He was looking down at the water, moving the heel of his boot gently over its surface. Eliav felt a sudden connection across the dark room, an intimate physical charge between himself and his father. He felt it as a tingling in his throat and his chest and he started sobbing.

Was the boy talking anymore? Were his father's eyes even open?

There was a boom and then a silence. A tight connection across all that space and then a snapping of that connection. A boom and then a body slumped over in a chair. Something heavy slung from bones.

He felt the explosion through the barrel, the double action in the chamber, the grip jerking upward. He felt it resonate in his hand, the ringing soreness in his shoulder.

There was a dark smear on his father's undershirt, an oblong stain partly covered by his head. There was the stillness of his father's hands. There were the shoelaces tied to his glasses, cutting a swath through the nearly bald skin at the back of his head.

———

For two thousand years, the Jews were not a race but a scattering, a dispersion. A multinational culture. It's what has always made us hated and feared, the perversity of having a culture without a land. No land that embodies the culture and is something to fight for, to die for. Only a weak, clever people could have devised such a culture. That was the way we were thought of for two thousand years.

— Reb Zvi Netanel, 2008

Fanatics, extremists. The kind of people Eliav had himself accused when I'd talked to him back in 2009. On the evening of December 22, 2008, two groups of young men abducted first Bellen and then Eliav, Bellen outside his apartment building on Levinsky Street, Eliav outside a 24-hour restaurant on the south side of Tel Aviv. They drove them separately to an abandoned storage facility in Bat Yam, where they tortured Bellen for three hours, then brought in Eliav. On July 27, 2012, the Judea and Samaria Division of the Israeli National Police arrested a twenty-two-year-old man named Sami Orlov, who was suspected of conspiring to explode a mosque in East Jerusalem. During his interrogation, Orlov confessed to his role in the Bellen murder three and a half years earlier. Sami Orlov is a follower of a rabbi named Zvi Netanel, who lives on an illegal outpost in the West Bank near Hebron. Netanel denies any connection to Sami Orlov or to Bellen's murder. But the goal of Netanel's movement, according to Netanel himself, is the restoration of a Jewish monarchy throughout the territory of the ancient one, a new Kingdom of David.

· It was Voss who told me the story. When he told me, I reminded him of Bellen's poem "Kid Bethlehem": *God is the small hard stone / in the boy's sling.*

"They're the fringe," Voss said. "Crazy people."

"It's not just Israel," I said. "That isn't what I meant. That's never been what I've meant."

The question of course was whether I was going to go back to Israel to do the assignment. The Sami Orlov assignment. It was July of 2012 and I had just filed the James Holmes assignment, the one about the psychotic student in Aurora, Colorado, who'd gone into a movie theater with a private arsenal and full body armor during a *Batman* premiere and shot seventy people, killing twelve of them. I was tired of such assignments, tired of such personalities. I told Voss about the strange vision I'd had in Jerusalem of the Hilltop Youth, those boys in their cargo pants marching David Bellen across the rocky field. How my fascination now seemed to me more than just a fascination. How it seemed more like an identification. How I somehow saw a part of myself not only in Bellen but in those boys — in their anger, in their thirst for extremes. How it seemed to me that someone else could perfectly well do the Sami Orlov story and I could be free of it.

As for Voss, he's coming to New York in a few days. Maybe we'll take a walk through my old neighborhood on the Upper East Side, his hand in mine, our backs to the traffic on Lexington as we leave the subway and pass the Starbucks, the shoe repair, the wine shop, the Korean deli with its newspapers and sunflowers. We'll go to the temple on 79th Street where I first met my teacher, Gila, then a few blocks down and across the street to my father's old antiques shop, its green awnings now replaced by the blue awnings of a national vitamin and health-food chain. I'll show him Gila's old apartment on 75th Street, the signs for H. KOTZ MEDICAL SUPPLIES and SYLVIE'S EUROPEAN ALTERATIONS still there, the block still like a vestige of some other time — my grandparents' time, Meyer Lansky's time, the block like an echo of the Brownsville slum where all their American stories began. Then I'll take Voss to the safe white building I grew up in on East End Avenue, its doorman and its boxwoods and its dwarf cherry trees, then finally we'll take a cab back across town to my current, equally safe life in Chelsea.

If I go back to Israel, I tell Voss, it won't be to do the Sami Orlov story.

If I go back, it won't even be for Voss.

If I go back to Israel, it will have to be for reasons of my own.

Acknowledgments

Most of the quotations from the Bible come from Robert Alter's *The David Story: A Translation with Commentary of 1 and 2 Samuel.* As a source on organized crime in Israel, Douglas Century's series "Holy Land Gangland" in the online magazine *Tablet* was of great value. My experience in Israel was enormously enhanced by the warm welcome given me by Maya Roman, Ellen Spolsky, and Marcela Sulak, among others. For their support while writing this book, I would like to thank the John Simon Guggenheim Memorial Foundation and Princeton University for its Hodder Fellowship. For their help and advice along the way, I would like to thank John Dalton, Jameson Ellis, Joshua Ferris, Mary Jo Bang, Peter Ho Davies, Marshall Klimasewiski, Edmund White, Bill Clegg, Pat Strachan, Victoria Matsui, and most of all my wife, Sarah.

About the Author

Zachary Lazar is the author of three previous books, including the novel *Sway*, chosen as a Best Book of 2008 by the *Los Angeles Times*, *Rolling Stone*, *Publishers Weekly*, and *Newsday*, and the memoir *Evening's Empire: The Story of My Father's Murder*, a *Chicago Tribune* Best Book of 2009. Lazar is the recipient of a Guggenheim Fellowship and the Hodder Fellowship at Princeton University. He lives in New Orleans, where he is on the creative writing faculty at Tulane University.